COSMIC
DESIRES

*Naughty stories of the
sci-fi and paranormal kind*

JESSICA E. SUBJECT

CONTENTS

TAKEN BY THE BILLIONAIRE ALIEN NEXT DOOR

Moving into a new home always proves stressful, but moving into a mansion bigger than all the houses I've ever lived in combined left my head spinning. Growing up, I had daydreamed with my mother about her marrying a billionaire, but I'd never expected it to happen. And I didn't reckon she would meet him while working at a museum of used props and costumes from old sci-fi television shows and movies. I mean, the geeks who filled the place failed to notice the cleavage showing in her low-cut tops. But, she did meet her billionaire, and I'd just unpacked the last box of the day of my belongings in my new bedroom in his house, a space with a closet and bathroom each larger than the last room I'd called my own. The best birthday present ever. As of today, I was legal to drink, vote, and everything in between in every state.

I didn't plan to live in Stephan's house for long, especially since my mother didn't need me to help her pay rent any longer. But Stephan had insisted I stay, at least until I finished community college, since continuing my education hadn't been an option before Mom met him.

Breaking down all the empty boxes, I groaned at the thought of having to interact with my new stepbrother, thirty-year-old Barron, a six-foot-two douche bag who still lived at home. Sure, he worked for his father's investment firm, but he had more than enough money to live on his own, a fact he rubbed in my face the few times we'd met. Otherwise, he'd never said much else, giving me the evil eye over dinner, as if I tried to take his fortune away. Hardly! I wanted my mom to be happy, and Stephan Gaskill managed to do that.

Though, I wouldn't experience their joy for the next month, since Barron happened to be my only company while the happy couple toured Europe on their honeymoon. Sure, the house had a staff of twenty, but they all had their own duties excluding keeping me company.

I gathered the flattened boxes and headed out of my room, to put them in the trunk of my car. But I needed to park the convertible Stephan had given me—a welcome-to-the-family gift—in the garage at the far end of the property. And I didn't have a remote—the one my new stepfather ordered had not arrived yet. Which meant hunting down my stepbrother for his. After sending him a quick text, I waited for his answer. The house had an intercom system, but it didn't reach every room. I figured a direct text would be the fastest and easiest way to get in contact with him. Five minutes passed and no answer came. He either didn't have his phone on him or was ignoring me. I assumed the second option, given how welcoming he had been when I'd pulled up earlier in the day with my belongings. The simple text he'd sent then had said, *Door is open. Your room is at the top of the stairs.* Nice. Great company for the next thirty days.

Not wanting to leave the car outside with dark clouds looming, I shoved the boxes back in my room and headed out in search of Barron. I walked the east and west wings

2

of the house, peeking inside open doors and putting my ear to the closed ones. Nothing. Returning to my room, I caught the scent of something delicious wafting up from the main floor. It reminded me of my grandmother's house, where fresh-baked food had never been in short supply. If she hadn't passed away before I'd turned eight, I would weigh three times what I did. Following my nose to the kitchen, I found one of the house staff busy cooking, I guessed our dinner, a meal Stephan insisted be eaten in the formal dining room.

I didn't know the cook's name, but he nodded and smiled. "Can I help you, Miss Erika?"

"Yes, I um.... Do you happen to know where Barron is?"

"Probably next door with Master Laken." He shook his head. "He spends most of his time over there. I'm not sure he even sleeps here anymore."

"What does he do next door?" And why did rich kids stay at home so long? If I hadn't felt obligated to help my mom, I would have moved out at eighteen. Maybe Barron and his friend still liked to geek out on video games, or maybe they were secret lovers?

"Heavens if I know. Though, while I feel sorry for the staff at the Montgomery's, I enjoy the hours when Master Barron is not around."

Interesting. I wasn't the only one who'd clashed with Barron. "Am I allowed over there? I have something quick to ask him and he's not answering his phone."

"Is there anything I can help you with?"

"Um, I need a key to the garage." I shrugged. "I don't suppose you have one."

"No, but I can call over to Bianca, the Montgomery's chef. She can let you in and point you in the right direction."

I clasped my hands together. "That would be great."

Staring out the kitchen window over to the Montgomery's, I tried not to eavesdrop on the man's conversation. The monstrous house appeared the same size as Stephan's, too big for only four people. Did all rich people live the same, with so much space they didn't have to interact with each other? And meeting Barron's friends held little appeal, not if they acted anything like him.

"Okay, you're good to go." The man tucked away his cell phone. "Head out the back door and follow the garden path over to the Montgomery's."

"Thank you." I exited the house, determined to find my stepbrother, bug him the way any sister should her brother. I had so many years to make up for.

"Be sure to tell Master Barron dinner will be served in an hour. It would be nice if you were both at the table this evening."

"Okay," I called over my shoulder. I hurried along the garden path, wanting to get the car parked indoors before the first raindrop fell. Though I doubted Barron would join me for the meal.

A pretty woman about the same age as our cook met me at the Montgomery's back door. Bianca? If so, I'm sure she traded more than recipes with our cook. "Miss Erika, it's great to meet you. I hope you are adjusting to your new home."

"Thank you." I curtsied, not sure where the instinct came from. "I just have a question for Barron if you can help me track him down."

"Sure." She led me to a set of stairs. "Down there to Master Laken's private area, where he likes to entertain friends."

"Thank you." I nodded this time and followed the steps down. Find Barron and go. I didn't want to be in anyone's *private area*, especially when I didn't know them.

In the first room on the lower level, what I assumed to be the den, not a single soul existed. If he spent all his time in the lower level, it wasn't in this room. Turned off, the flat-screen television sported a thin layer of dust, with a giant family portrait hanging on an angle above it. The picture must have been taken years ago, when the children had been in their early teens, not adults as I assumed they would be.

A faint hum came from my left, a noise reminding me of the constantly running factory a block away from where I used to live. Maybe it would lead me in the right direction.

As I traipsed down the hall past a multitude of closed white doors, the sound grew louder. But unlike the noise from the factory, this was a higher-pitched sound, almost like a song. I followed the hall as it veered to the right, a steel door at the end. Not inconspicuous at all. It had a simple lock on it, no keypad or anything complicated. So, what lay behind it couldn't be very valuable. Probably a maintenance room containing the furnace and other equipment to run the monstrous house. Since the latch hadn't caught and the door stood open a crack, I pushed it wider and peeked inside.

I spotted a guy who could be my stepbrother. Except he had dark hair and stood naked, save for a pair of tight silver shorts. Skin the color of golden honey covered wave upon wave of tight muscle. A flash of warmth washed over me as I imagined licking him all over, going down on my knees in front of him to find out if he tasted as sweet as he appeared.

Sure, I shouldn't fantasize about a stranger, but I couldn't help myself. Barron wasn't around, and this guy exuded sex appeal. A god compared to the strung-out sleazebags I'd had to choose from in high school. Maybe I craved some attention since I only had seven more hours before my birthday ended. A day I'd spent by myself, while my friends worked or took care of their brand-new babies.

But, I wouldn't have to be alone if I approached the eye candy in front of me and ripped off his tight shorts and discovered what hid underneath. Touch and taste and.... Oh, God! I crossed my legs, trying to ignore the throbbing of my pussy.

I sucked in a deep breath in an effort to gain control over my body. Could the hottie in front of me be Laken? And if so, where had Barron disappeared to? Changing my focus, I glanced beyond the guy's luscious body to see what captivated his attention.

With delicate movements, he traced his finger across intricate black patterns on the large, round steel object in front of him, part of a...a....

I stared, unable to move. I think my heart paused for a beat or two while my mind tried to digest the bulky mass in the center of the room.

A spaceship. An honest-to-goodness flying saucer. I gasped. If a model, its creator had designed a damn realistic one with perfect angles and the occasional dent. Maybe from impact with space debris. On the other side of the room, sliding metal doors, heavy chains keeping them closed.

The guy studying the craft spun around, rigid, as if in shock.

I jumped back, not only at being caught, but because of his eyes. They were black. All black. No white, no irises, just a glossy black.

I spun to leave, but the guy moved faster than any human should be able to, appearing in front of me before I made it out the door.

"Who are you? What are you doing here? And why...?" He sounded normal though, seemed like any other hot, red-blooded American.

"Erika." As I glanced down to avoid his creepy stare, a war broke out inside me. I couldn't help but notice his washboard abs and the large bulge in the front of his shorts. If not for the inhuman eyes and crazy-ass speed, I would jump him right there, no questions asked. "I'm Barron's stepsister. Is he here?"

"No, who told you he would be?"

"Bianca?" My voice came out in a squeaky whisper.

"Of course." He sighed. Actually sighed.

I dared a peek at his face again. His eyes looked normal this time, or mostly. His irises were a light blue, almost white, a color I had never seen before in humans, and they stood out even more in contrast to his wavy, dark-brown hair. But they weren't black, which made me wonder if I'd imagined the whole thing. Maybe a trick of the light? But nothing explained his speed, or the spaceship. I glanced over my shoulder to ensure it still sat there. Yep. One flying saucer in the basement of a billionaire's house.

"Your brother's not here."

"Stepbrother," I said automatically, returning my attention to Mr. Sexy. "Now, tell me, who are you?" I wanted to add *what are you*, but thought better of it.

"I am Laken."

"Then where is Barron?" For a brief moment, I worried about my new stepbrother. "What have you done with him?"

The sigh again, as if I'd asked the dumbest question.

Laken shook his head. "He's with my sister." Placing his palm on the wall, he leaned against it and crossed his ankles. "Always says he's coming over here to hang out with me then takes off with her. I only cover for him because I'd rather have both of them out of my hair. I prefer to be alone."

"So you can study the spaceship?" If not for the strange abnormalities, I'd assume him a science geek who'd built a giant model of some ship from a sci-fi show. But, no.

"Spaceship?"

"Yes, the one behind me." I crossed my arms. He couldn't pretend it didn't exist. The thing occupied half the room, at least fifteen feet in diameter, the space obviously designed to hold the craft.

"I, uh.... You don't...?"

Confused? Cute, but it didn't work on me. "Your sister, is she like you?" And did Barron know? Because I couldn't imagine him seeing anyone who wasn't rich, beautiful, *and* human.

He frowned. "Like me? You mean—"

God, I hated the playing-stupid routine. "Yeah, with the all black eyes, speediness, and such."

"What exactly do you think I am, Miss Erika?"

"An alien." There, I'd said it, and I expected him to laugh in my face and deny it.

Instead, he placed his hands behind his back and stepped nearer. "And what if I am?"

My breath caught. "I...." I should have kept my mouth shut. No, I should have waited for Barron to text a reply, never come over to the neighbor's house. Now, I was stuck in a basement hangar with a flying saucer and a guy who could be from another planet.

Laken inched closer, and closer still. I moved along with him until my back hit a wall on the other side of the room. Trapped. Trying to duck away wouldn't do me any good. He'd only race around and block my way again. My heart beat so hard, I expected it to thump right out of my chest. Would he let me go, or did he have other plans? If I screamed loud enough, would someone come to my rescue?

Leaning forward, he placed his palm on the wall behind me. "What if I told you I knew the instant you came into this room?" He ran his other hand along my cheekbone, tucking my hair behind an ear. "What if I told you I could feel your attraction, smell your sex?"

A shiver raced down my spine. Sure, I wanted to jump his bones before I'd seen his eyes. Now, I yearned for a way out, a clear path to escape from Mr. Sex-on-a-stick who may or may not be an extraterrestrial.

He dipped his head so close to mine, his warm breath brushed my neck. A flash of heat washed over me. Fuck, it had been so long since I'd been with any guy. Did it really matter where he came from?

"What if, Erika? If I am an alien? Would you still find me attractive? Would you still want to lick me from head to toe? Suck my cock? Would you want me to fuck you against this wall, in my spaceship, and on every single surface of this room?"

If not for him sliding his knee between my thighs, I would have melted into a puddle of lust at that moment. Who was I trying to kid? I had the hots for an extraterrestrial. I wanted to do everything he said, craved to feel his alien cock thrusting in and out of my pussy. Running away wouldn't work, and wouldn't satisfy my aching need.

I cupped the bulge in his pants. "Yes, I want all of that." I'd never had the opportunity to be fucked by a man of his caliber. Whether he came from Earth or beyond, I wanted to experience him.

Laken grasped my wrists, raising my hands above my head. Pressing his groin against me, he kissed along my jawline until his lips met mine. Hard, demanding, he plunged his tongue in my mouth, claiming it the way I wanted him to claim the rest of my body.

Releasing my wrists, he slid his hands down my arms, my sides, resting them on my hips. Synapses fired under my skin, demanding more from him. I pulled him even closer and wrapped a leg around his thigh. All worries about where he came from fled, lust remaining the only thing on my mind.

After cinching the skirt of my dress up, he leaned down and gripped the cheeks of my ass. His lips separated from mine for an instant, but enough to draw in a deep breath. God, I'd never expected to get fucked against the wall by a stranger when I'd walked into the Montgomery home, but now I didn't want to leave before it happened.

He lifted me, pinning me even tighter to the wall. I wrapped my legs around his waist, craving him closer, wishing the clothes between us would disappear so he could ram right into me.

Reaching between my legs from behind, he yanked my thong to the side, exposing my throbbing pussy. So close. I wanted to shake him, make him drop me so I could yank off his tiny shorts before hopping onto his glorious cock and going for a ride. But when he drew his finger across my clit, I shuddered.

Yes! Bright lights danced behind my closed eyes. I rocked across his finger, savoring what he offered.

"Hold onto me."

I snapped to attention, surprised by his sexy baritone voice. I'd forgotten what he sounded like. Clutching my wrists behind his neck, I did as he'd asked. Then he released me. If I hadn't had a tight hold, I would have crashed to the ground.

Hard lines of determination formed on his forehead as he worked around me to remove his shorts. I had to cross my ankles behind his back, losing my grip when he wiggled to get free from his clothing. After kicking the material across the room, he pinned me to the wall again. He kissed along my neck, down my chin, reigniting the rush of desire. The tip of his cock brushed along my labia. So close. Dangerously close. Fuck, what was I thinking?

"Laken, stop."

He rested his forehead on mine and stared into my eyes. Black again, but I refused to run. "What do you mean? You want to leave?"

I gripped the back of his head. "No! God, no. Maybe pause is a better word."

His cock flexed, and I jumped as it pushed through my entrance. Way too close.

I shimmied my hands between us and shoved his shoulder. "Condom." Lowering my feet to the ground, I planted my hands on his chest and pushed him back. "This isn't going any further until you put a condom on. I don't care who or what you are."

Sure, I used birth control pills to prevent pregnancy, but I didn't want some freaky disease from the alien next door.

He squeezed his eyes shut then opened them wide, as if

hoping to make them look human again. But they remained a glossy black.

"Listen." I stepped closer and gripped his balls, rubbing the heel of my hand along the base of his cock. "I think you're hot, regardless of what you are. I want you to fuck me, but we need to use some form of protection."

"Okay." He nodded and placed a hand on my shoulder, squeezing gently.

A tingle spread through my body, beginning where his palm rested on my skin. Nothing like our desperate passion. Something different. More like frigid water rushing through my veins. When the sensation reached the tips of my fingers and toes, I disappeared. No other way to describe it. I stood there with Laken, and then I was gone, floating in nothingness. But, only for a few seconds. When I returned, I'd left the hangar.

Giant pillows covered in black satin cradled my naked body, my dress and undergarments having been left behind somewhere. Laken lay to my right, propping his head in one hand and brushing hair from my face with the other.

I pushed up onto my elbows. "Where are we?"

The circular room smelled of steel, but I couldn't see beyond the dark plush curtains hanging around the large...bed?

"In my room. I had to bring you here for protection."

"Yes, but how?" I drew in a sharp breath as he circled a finger around my nipple. It took every ounce of concentration to focus on my thoughts rather than his ministrations. "We were in that hangar room one second, and the next we were here. And I'm naked."

"Because I am what you believe me to be." He rolled onto me, pressing me deeper into the soft pillows. His knee between my thighs, he captured my lips in a hard kiss, sucking, plunging his tongue into my mouth, like our session in the hangar had never ended.

Yearning to clear some things up before I got it on with an extraterrestrial, I turned my head to the side.

"Hold up." I stared into his black eyes, examining them for the first time, knowing what I saw wasn't my imagination playing tricks on me. "You really are an alien? Like, from outer space?" I had to be sure, not feel like a fool when I learned my assumptions were incorrect.

He rolled back to my side. "Yes."

The curtain surrounding us parted, and with a whoosh, a panel folded out, opening to another room. No, not another room. We were still inside the hangar, but inside the spaceship. I was in a flying saucer.

Laken gestured toward the opening. "You can leave if you wish."

An invisible weight pushed on my chest. "You want me to leave?" Sure, I barely knew him, but in no way did I have any urge to leave. And it hurt to think he might wish me gone.

"No." He rolled onto his back, resting his hands behind his head. "But if you can't handle what I am, you're more than welcome to go back home."

I glanced out the door then back at him. He'd known my thoughts when I'd first noticed him, so he should have known what I hoped for then. Closing my eyes, I visualized what I yearned to do to him, what I craved for him to do to me.

He groaned, and I opened my eyes when his fingers dug into my hip bone. The ship's door had already closed, and the curtains swung shut. Laken's mouth hung open and his cock jutted straight up, ready for what I'd pictured.

Crawling between his spread legs, I grasped its base. So freakin' hard, I couldn't wait to feel him inside me. But first, I wanted a taste.

With gentle pressure, I eased the foreskin down to expose the swollen head. Bending over him, I ran my tongue over the tip. Spicy, like nutmeg and cinnamon. At his quiet moan, I grinned. So empowering to have an extraterrestrial from some unknown planet at my mercy.

Staring up at the enigma he was, I engulfed the entire

tip.

He bucked his hips. "Sweet heavens," he hissed through his teeth.

When I took his whole cock in my mouth, he growled, the noise echoing around the spacecraft.

As I bobbed up and down, he thrust to meet me, never afraid to vocalize his pleasure. I'd never been with a noisy lover. But then, we weren't trying to hide what we were doing from parents or roommates.

The muscles in his legs tightened. His cock swelled even more, nearly doubling in thickness. Ready to blow, and he hadn't even fucked me yet. He'd be asleep in a matter of minutes. Oh well. I could only hope for an invitation to return. I clutched his slippery shaft in my hand and stroked, jerking him off until he released.

As the dark, sticky liquid shot across his chest, Laken jerked and twitched with an eerie silence. Had I done something wrong? Hurt him somehow?

I ran a hand over his thigh. "Are you okay?"

His eyelids flicked open, one eye black and the other human looking, with that piercing clear-blue color. One or the other I could handle, but not one of each. I crawled backward until I hit the curtain.

"Wait!" He sat up, his body clean, as if his skin had absorbed his release. "It's your turn."

He grabbed my ankles and yanked me across the pillows toward him. My feet were in the air and his tongue buried in my pussy before I had any chance to speak—though I had no objections. He hadn't fallen asleep after his release and seemed anxious to pleasure me, so I didn't dare say a word. I gripped the black satin, reveling in each swirl of his tongue, the way the muscle seemed to fold over itself, flicking my clit at the same time he thrust inside. The perks of being an alien? Or was he just plain gifted? I had no time to consider, desire pooling low in my belly. Heat flared across my skin. I erupted in a flash of euphoria, synapses firing from head to toe.

Reaching up my body, he pinched my nipples, sending another wave of rapture through me. I tilted my head back, longing for a deep breath and for my heart to stop pounding.

At the sound of crinkling plastic, I glanced around for him. It took me a few seconds to focus, but I found him to my left, tearing open a condom package. Pinching the tip, he rolled the thin latex over his shaft, obviously not a stranger to how they worked. Had he been with a lot of women from Earth? Did they all know his secret, too? Oh God, what if he fucked them then killed them to keep anyone else from finding out?

A gust of wind blew across my face. Laken kneeled between my legs, and used his strength to hold my arms above my head. "Jealousy and fear are very unbecoming for you."

Shit. He couldn't read my thoughts, but he'd come pretty damn close to sensing my emotions. I used to dream my boyfriends had such an ability. Now, I wasn't so sure I liked the invasion into my mind. "But, how many—"

"One." He ran his tongue along my jawline before nibbling the skin below my ear. My worries disappeared. My thoughts vanished. Delirium set in.

"I've only had one lover," he whispered in between his sensual assault on my neck. "We parted ways a few months back. She signed a contract to keep my secret, and I signed one to keep the secrets of her family."

His mouth left my skin, and he stared down at me, the tip of his cock resting outside my entrance. "The same way I will keep yours."

Mine? I didn't have any secrets. At least none he would know after meeting me less than an hour earlier. "But—"

He plunged, stealing away the rest of my words. *So thick.* I didn't think he'd have room to move. Full, I felt unbelievably full. Yet, I experienced no pain. Only a heightened sensitivity to his every motion.

"You're like me, Erika." He managed gentle strokes,

pushing deeper with each one. "I knew from the moment you stepped into my hangar."

"No." The word came out in a whimper, not because of what he'd said, but I didn't think I could handle any more of his cock inside of me, my head ready to explode from the buildup of energy. I couldn't concentrate on his words, what he had told me, only the fullness immersed in my core. The urge to push him out battled with the desire for more. I held on tight to his biceps, unable to control the increasing pressure.

Laken grabbed my hips and thrust harder. Faster, burying himself until he could go no farther. He lifted my legs onto his shoulders and pounded my pussy. The tension never let up. I yearned for release, my body ready to burst into flames.

"C'mon, baby. It's time to come for me." Switching to long, slow strokes, he brushed his thumb over my clit— the spark I needed.

I cried out as the waves of ecstasy took hold. Gripping the cushions around me, I writhed under him. He never let up, continued to grind in and out, keeping me in a state of bliss. I'd never come down from such a high before, yet still couldn't find the ground. I abandoned the search, heading for another release.

He held my thighs against his chest and drove his cock. Jolts of pleasure raced through me as I detonated for a second time. Electric tension like no other.

Laken groaned with his own release, his magnificent body shuddering. "Oh, Er-i-ka."

When he stopped convulsing, he lowered my legs and leaned down to kiss me. The urgency and lust were gone, his lips filled with passion, as if we weren't strangers. Like we'd made love hundreds of time before.

Made love? No. I barely knew him. He was an alien. A billionaire alien, for fuck's sake. And me, a poor girl who had a new, rich stepfather. But, I could never change where I came from.

Laken kissed my nose, my forehead, my cheeks, slipping out of me. "Gods, that felt so good, to be with someone of my kind."

I missed the pressure of him inside me. Shaking my head, I pushed the emptiness aside and focused on what he had said. "Your kind?" He'd admitted being from another planet. But, I wasn't. Nope, born and raised in a public housing development. Not Tent City, but nothing like the gated community we lived in now. And definitely not another planet.

"Yes, your father—"

"Was never around." I tried to push Laken off, but he held tight. "He fucked my mom and left the next morning, said he'd grab them some breakfast but never returned."

"His name was Andreas." He brushed a piece of hair from my forehead, ignoring my objections. "He came to Earth with my family. But the government discovered him. Probably the morning after you were conceived."

Impossible. My father was a good-for-nothing asshole who'd used my mother and tossed her away when he'd gotten what he wanted, not some space traveler stolen away before he knew he would be a father.

Laken said, "My parents tried to locate him, rescue their friend from the compound where the government held him. But, by the time they found him, he was dead."

A lump formed in my throat. "No."

"He would have made a wonderful father. And, you kind of look like him."

My heart slammed against my ribs, trying to escape. Tears burned the corners of my eyes. "Then why didn't—"

"Shh." He wiped my cheeks. "No one knew he'd conceived a child. Otherwise, my parents would have brought your mother here to live with us, help raise you. But, I recognized your soul the moment I turned around. It's the reason I can read you so well."

"You're making this up." Somehow, he'd tapped into my psyche, feeding me what I'd wanted to hear my entire life. Or something like it. A story that made my father out to be a hero rather than a piece of dog shit.

"Can't you sense it?" Still keeping his weight on me, he reached over for another condom, taking the old one off and replacing it with a new one. He licked the skin between my breasts then ran his tongue up my boob to circle my nipple. "Can't you feel our connection?"

When he slid back inside, I felt whole again, but not because my father came from another planet. I simply enjoyed sex. With Laken.

"You don't need to make shit up to fuck me." I wrapped my leg around his, knocking him off balance and onto his back. Bracing my hands on his shoulders, I eased back onto his cock. "Please don't feed me any more lies."

He was the best fuck I'd ever had, but it would never happen again. This would be my last orgasm with him and I planned to make it the best one yet. I rocked my hips, focusing on nothing but my driving hunger, the bottomless ache for another release. My mind whirled each time his dick hammered my G-spot.

Heaven! The electric tension barreled through me, a spiraling end to our time together. His cock swelled right before he crested. He pulled me down to his chest, holding me tight as he emptied his seed. Thank goodness I'd insisted on a condom. Who knew what the crazy alien might have spread to me if I hadn't? Or maybe he wasn't an alien at all, just skilled at creating illusions.

I struggled free from his arms, ready to find my clothes and head home. Never would I take the path through the garden to the Montgomery's again.

Laken didn't stir, didn't say a word. But, burning tingles ran up and down my spine as he watched my every movement.

Crawling to the edge of the array of pillows, I brushed the curtains aside. The door remained closed. I rose to my feet and palmed the cold, gray steel, hoping to push it ajar.

A white light flashed in front of me. Temporarily

blinded, I blinked hard, trying to regain my vision. Instead of the wall of the spaceship, long, brown grass blew across an open field. Far in the distance, the sun glinted off a large object partly embedded in the ground. Seven black inky figures sauntered toward me, their forms becoming clearer with each step. Two were smaller—children hanging onto the hand of an adult. One of the tall figures limped behind, struggling to keep up with the others. Who were they and what did they have to do with me? Cold steel met my palm, making the vision just that—a vision. A gift from Laken or the ship itself?

I focused on the children, curious to understand who they were, why they existed in my delusion. A boy and a girl, both around eight or nine, they had dark, wavy hair, the boy's much shorter, feathered around his forehead and ears. Familiar. I'd seen them both not long ago. Yes! In the den on the way to the hangar. The family from the portrait. Laken and his sister, their parents holding their hands.

Then I noticed their eyes. All black. All seven pairs. Alien. They wore silver jumpsuits, the material dirty and ripped in places. Was this the day they had arrived on Earth? The day they'd crash landed? The Montgomerys and...?

I didn't recognize the woman or the man beside the family. But they vanished, everyone from the vision except the man limping. My stomach twisted. I hadn't seen him clearly before, blocked by the others, but now I could not mistake his identity.

Oh God, Laken hadn't lied. A tear trickled down my cheek. I'd always thought I looked like my mother. Not anymore. I was built like my father, compact up top, with long legs. We shared the same nose and chin, the same straight, walnut-colored hair.

The man had a large gash covering his right thigh, his injury slowing him down. My mom had mentioned playing nurse to my father the night she'd met him. I'd tuned out, not wanting to hear about their kinky sex. Yet, she hadn't meant it that way at all.

I reached out to him, yearning to help him, talk to the man I'd never known. But I couldn't push past the edge of the ship. The vision faded and I fell back on my ass, my head spinning from the revelation about my father. About myself and what I was.

Strong arms surrounded me, pulled me against a warm chest. Laken kissed the top of my head. He never said a word, simply held me as I shook and sobbed, my heart breaking. My father, stolen away from my mom and me.

When the tears subsided, I crawled off his lap, embarrassed by my blubbering outburst. Like he wanted to be a part of that.

Feather-soft kisses danced across my shoulders. He rubbed my arms from behind. "I'm so sorry."

I spun. "Don't be. I'm glad I finally know the truth. My dad wasn't a deadbeat." Just dead.

Laken traced his finger along the back of my hand. "No, he was a well-respected member of our crew."

Gazing into his dark eyes, I let the last of my sorrow wash away. "Will you tell me about him tomorrow?"

"What I remember, sure, but why not right now?"

I checked my watch. "Because I have about five minutes before I'm expected back home for dinner." Leaning forward, I pushed on his chest, knocking him back on the pillows. "But first—"

Laken yanked me down on top of him before flipping me onto my back. "I'm going to fuck my alien girlfriend."

"Girlfriend?" I'd only met him, but after the recent revelation, I couldn't imagine being with anyone else.

"Yep." He reached for another condom then rolled it over his cock. "We might as well have some fun while I teach you all the things you can do."

I didn't care what I could do at that moment. I wanted him inside me, craved the connection. One person to another. One alien to another. Spreading my legs, I grasped his hips and tugged him toward me. As his cock slid into me, I sighed. Pure bliss.

I'd begun the day a stranger in a new neighborhood, a new life. But, by the end, I'd found myself, and a hot, alien boyfriend.

Laken held me tight, gently rocking his hips. And we kissed. No desperation. Only passion. A deeper bond than I'd ever imagined possible in such a short time. Our bodies moved in sync and I reveled in the intoxicating rapture before surrendering to divine ecstasy.

REPLICATED CONSEQUENCES

Darryl sank into his chair, form-fitted by age. With his foot, he brushed the papers and dishes on the ottoman to the floor. He winced at the crash, but had little motivation to clean it up or do anything. Stretching out his legs, he rested them atop the cleared surface and closed his eyes. Opening them meant he would see her again, dressed in her pressed and polished uniform or naked with him in bed. But the memories of Beth simply fucked with his head. She was gone forever. Nothing he said or did would ever bring her back.

He cringed at the abrupt stabbing pain in his chest. No one said living with a broken heart was easy. He'd known the risks of dating her, but his awareness did nothing to prepare him for the agony of losing her.

Though a military woman marrying a civilian remained a rare occurrence at Beth's base, they'd celebrated their seventh anniversary four months ago, right before she deployed for the last time.

A knock interrupted his memories. Darryl flicked his eyes open and stared at the door. Perspiration beaded his skin. The last time someone had knocked—most rang the doorbell—bad news had followed. Two weeks ago. And he'd holed up inside ever since, only emerging for Beth's funeral.

He set his feet on the floor before walking on wobbly legs toward the entrance. What dark tidings would he receive?

Palms slick from sweat, he turned the knob. Catching sight of the two people on his stoop, he stepped back with a startled gasp. No way the people standing in front of him existed. He had to be dreaming.

The man in full military dress gave him a quick nod. "Mr. Malloy?"

He swallowed, his throat suddenly dry. "Yes."

"I have a delivery for you." The man touched the woman's back, ushering her forward. "She's all yours. Take care of her."

She? His? But.... Beth had died. He'd watched her body lowered into the ground, received the country's flag. No way could his wife be standing there. "There must be some mistake. Beth died."

Strolling down the walkway, the man paused and glanced back at him. "That's not Sergeant Malloy. It's her clone."

Hardly an *it*. Rather a copy of his wife. Darryl griped the doorjamb. His mind spun. Human cloning had just become public knowledge. And those created remained the property of the military. "Shouldn't she be in a lab somewhere? Or training for a mission?"

The man, at his parked Humvee, shook his head. "We had special instructions to bring her here should anything happen to the sergeant."

Darryl rubbed the back of his neck, studying the woman in his care. While she resembled his late wife in every way, from her tight bun to her sexy pout, he had no idea what to do with her. "So, you're a clone?"

She tilted her head, pointing to the raised ring of skin on her long, creamy-white neck.

Darryl groaned, fighting the urge to lick her skin from her collarbone to the scar remaining from the removal of her information portal. She wasn't his wife, but that didn't matter to his libido. He craved her the same.

Not once had he strayed from his commitment to Beth. And when she'd arrived home after months away, they hadn't wasted any time reuniting . Even though he knew the clone wasn't his wife, his hormones raced.

With a brief smile, she glanced inside. "May I come in?"

In? To live with him? Taking Beth's place in bed? He could turn his studio into a second bedroom, but hadn't expected to have another person to worry about. At least not for some time. "I...I don't even know your name."

"I am B17." She leaned close. Her uniform covered breasts pressed against him. "But Beth always called me Bryn."

He sucked air through his teeth, and imagined lifting her by her ass to carry her straight to bed. He recognized the name, remembered Beth talking about her as if her best friend. Now he knew why his wife had never invited her over.

Clinging to his last ounces of control, he stepped aside and followed the sway of her curved ass. But she didn't tread very far, stopping inside the foyer.

"What's the meaning of this?"

He cringed at the sharp tone of her voice. "Of what?"

"This mess." She spun toward him, pinching her nose. "Did you have a party to celebrate Beth's death then let everything rot?"

"No!" Celebrate her death? Beth was his life. He still didn't know how to go on without her.

"Then what happened? How can you live in this filth?"

She set her hands on her hips and raised her eyebrows, tapping her toe.

Just the way his wife used to.

"I...." A lump formed in his throat. "It's been hard

these last two weeks. I've had a lot to deal with."

"I suppose you have." Her pursed lips offered little sympathy. "But Beth would not accept excuses. She would punish you if she saw this mess."

Punish. It seemed so long ago she'd last used the paddle on him. Perhaps he'd let their home become a mess, to give her a reason to come back to him. "Yes, she would."

"Then I will have to do it."

Blood rushed to his groin. His cock rose in anticipation. He didn't know what Bryn had in mind, but with Beth, pleasure always followed the sting of her punishments. "If you must."

She set her carry-on bag on the floor. Squatting, she reached inside and drew out a paddle longer than any Beth had ever used on him. Though wooden paddles did not come cheap, his wife owned one the size of a hairbrush. Her clone held one much bigger. At least sixteen inches long, and clear plastic riddled with holes to make the punishment sting more.

Bryn yanked on the elastic holding her hair up. Her caramel-colored locks fell past her shoulders. She unbuttoned her uniform to reveal a generous amount of cleavage and resembled a dominatrix of times past.

When she slapped the paddle across her palm, he groaned.

"You will clean up first." She inspected the small living room and kitchen. "One swat for every ten minutes it takes you to make it shine."

Ten minutes? His ass tingled. It would take at least an hour. Though likely much longer. "That's not fair. The mess didn't happen in a day."

"Then you'd better get started." She tapped the paddle to his ass. "I'm timing you."

Great! He wouldn't sleep on his back that night, lucky if he slept at all.

Beginning in the living room, he picked up all the garbage and dirty dishes. By the time he'd finished, the floors sparkled and the rotten smell was replaced by lemony freshness. Almost two hours had passed. Ten swats.

"Much better." Bryn nodded. "Now it's time for your punishment, to remind you to clean up after yourself."

He stripped and stood naked, hands behind his back and legs apart. He kept his gaze fixed on the floor lest more slaps be added to his high number.

"Over my lap."

Darryl groaned at the sudden change in her tone, from stern to sultry. What would she do to him after his spanking? He kneeled and lay over her lap, sure to touch the tip of his cock to her thigh. Yes, he deserved the punishment, but he craved so much more.

Bryn caressed the cheeks of his ass, her palms delicate, like Beth's. He'd never expected her to cause him any pain. Heck, he wouldn't have guessed her in the military when they'd first met. But she'd surprised him in many ways and made her expectations clear.

"Your ass is round and firm. It will glow nicely by the time I'm done."

Not the first time he'd heard the words. He yearned for her to stop playing with him and spank already.

Bryn reached between his legs. When she grabbed his shaft, he sucked in a breath and released it with a groan.

"Interesting. I've never met a guy so turned on by impending pain." She squeezed before releasing him. "Let's get started."

He braced for the first spank. No matter how often Beth had punished him, the first swat came as a surprise. With a different paddle, Bryn could inflict even more pain.

The plastic struck, setting his ass on fire. He shot forward with a yelp, unsure he'd get through all ten.

"I expect you to count." Bryn caressed his stinging skin, her touch absorbing some of the hurt.

"One." Darryl closed his eyes, waiting for the next.
Smack!

Another cry. "Two." His ass burned as if he sat on hot coals.

The next three followed in quick succession, the pain blinding. He'd barely caught his breath in between. Had he counted? But Bryn hadn't scolded him.

The paddle clanked on the table, and she grabbed his cock. "Not so excited anymore. I'm not sure if that's good or bad."

"I've learned my lesson." He rocked into her fist. The sting disappeared as desire surged.

Bryn let go. "I don't think you have. You just want what Beth gave you after. Not this time."

His muscles jerked with number six. All lust for the woman vanished. She wasn't his wife. Just a clone who wanted to punish him. He tried to roll away, but she gripped his side.

"If you leave, I'll add more."

"Then get them over with."

The next came so hard and fast, tears formed in the corners of his eyes. "Seven." He didn't want the woman there. She had no right to take Beth's place.

"Eight, nine, ten." She tapped out the last three. "I'm done."

Darryl tensed, sure she baited him.

She stroked his back and his ass, soothing the burn. "I can't do this anymore. I can't pretend to be her. Not with you." Gone was the confidence and command in her voice.

He slid from her lap and kneeled in front of her. "You don't have to be Beth. I don't expect you to."

She shook her head and glanced toward the windows. "No, I mean pretending to be Bryn, to be a clone."

He gripped the sides of her chair, shock rolling through him. "Beth?"

Chewing her bottom lip, she nodded.

Darryl stood and pulled her into his arms. Doubt crept in and he set her back on her feet. "But you deployed."

"No. Bryn went in my place." She clasped his hands. "I knew it was a suicide mission. She did, too."

"And you sent her?" Clone or not, she shouldn't have been sent to die.

"She kind of volunteered." Beth rubbed the side of her neck. "I didn't stand a chance when she tied me up and cut me so it would look like she'd removed my portal."

"What about hers? Didn't anyone notice?" He loved having his wife back, but didn't want anyone to learn her identity and take her away.

"They didn't even look." A tear slipped down her cheek. "She arranged everything, even for my clone to be released to you after my death. Said she was created to take my place in dangerous situations and must fulfill her purpose."

"And yet you came in here and spanked me?" Why hadn't she told him?

The sorrow gone, his strict military wife returned. "You deserved it. Bryn would have done the same thing. She's the one who taught me about spanking. Someone fed her that programming."

"I think you deserve a spanking for letting me believe you'd died." He cringed as soon as the words left his mouth, expecting Beth to demand punishment for his outburst. Instead, she smiled and cupped his testicles.

"Maybe. But we have some reuniting to do."

He scooped her into his arms and headed to their room. His wife was home. For good.

CRASH LANDING

Cael gripped the cushioned arms of the captain's chair as his ship tumbled bow over stern. The console flashed a blinding red in front of him. Piercing alarms drilled into his mind, and he lost focus. The seconds raced by as he plummeted toward Earth. He'd fucked up this mission of peace. Contact with his home planet had ended months ago. No one from Narien could save him now. His death was imminent.

The water below wouldn't soften his landing. At its current speed, his ship would disintegrate on splashdown. The planet's gravity pulled him down faster.

He coughed; the acrid scent of fried electronics stung his nose and the back of his throat. *Please let my death be quick.*

A rattling to the left caught his attention above all other noise. The handle on the cabin door shook. *Freedom.* It wasn't his time to die, *if* he could get out.

The altimeter on the dashboard read six thousand meters, high enough to jump and land safely with his chute. *Only to land in frigid water and die of exhaustion or hypothermia from treading without any hope of a rescue.*

"Shit." But he'd die for certain if he stayed. He had to take the chance. Yanking off his safety harness, he pulled himself to standing and strained to reach the recess where his pack hung. Stretching up, he fingered the cloth strap. Not close enough to grab hold of it.

The ship jolted and flung him to the stern. He weaved his arm through the straps of the pack on his way past, dislodging it from the hook. *Yes.*

His triumph was short-lived as he flew starboard, smashing his shoulder against the wall. He groaned when an electrifying spasm shot down his arm to the tips of his fingers. The ship lurched again, and he tumbled back toward the console. He grabbed the door, his feet dangling in mid air. If he didn't get out now, he'd forfeit any chance to survive.

The ship righted again. He planted his feet against the bottom of the door and twisted the crank. The latch snapped open, filling him with a sense of hope. Careful to keep at least one hand on the handle at all times, he slung the pack over his shoulders.

All set. Time to jump. Pushing off the floor, he slammed his uninjured shoulder against the door. It blew open and tore away from its hinges, lost to the sky.

Cael teetered on the edge before plunging out of his failing ship. Wind whipped all around him as he twisted to catch his bearings during freefall.

Glancing down, he spied a crystal blue lake, much closer than he'd expected. *Too close.*

He jerked the cord on his chute—several hundred feet lower than he should have. At least. His feet skimmed the cold waves just as his chute caught the current and heaved him back into the air.

The ship splashed into the water beside him, disintegrating into millions of pieces. He raised his hands in front of his face as shrapnel flew at him. Tiny shards sliced into his arms and legs, but the extreme heat from the cloud of steam billowing up at him stung the most.

From the moment his toes touched down in the once frigid water, his skin sizzled. He screamed in agony. His death would have been quicker and less agonizing if he'd remained in the ship.

A hard piece of his spacecraft smashed down on his head, and he welcomed the darkness.

Cael flicked his eyes open and stared at his surroundings: a room made from timber, like some of the Terran dwellings he'd studied before travelling to Earth. Did the afterlife resemble the blue and green planet?

Sitting up, he yelped in agony. No, he was very much alive. He glanced across his body, naked except for white gauze covering his dark blue feet, arms, and a patch on his lower abdomen. Someone had rescued him and bandaged his wounds. But who? And why? He didn't look like anyone on the planet, his skin a foreign color. And laboratories were supposed to be cold and reek of cleaners. This room smelled organic, and he had no complaints about the temperature.

He swung his legs over the edge of the platform. More pain shot through his body. Lying down again, he hoped the soreness would lessen. But no.

His ears rang, and the hollows behind his eyes ached, echoing the throbbing in his head. Would the beings in this place make him suffer through the hurt?

Hands pressed down on him, against his legs and across his forehead. He struggled against them, but the suffering had left him weak. He'd been warned some Terrans would not welcome a space traveler. Glancing from side to side, he only saw shadows, no features on the faces staring down at him. Maybe he'd been wrong in believing Earthlings would bring him no harm. He needed to get away, escape before they killed him as the pain intensified. But his body remained out of his control. He couldn't focus on anything. Voices spoke to him through the pounding in his head, but he couldn't comprehend their words. Something sharp pierced his arm, and a warm liquid emptied into his veins. This was it. His end. Again.

Cael gasped, bolting upright. He peeked around the room, the same place he'd woken before. He swept off the sheet covering him. All of his bandages had been removed, leaving only slight scarring on his blue skin. He stretched his arms into the air, surprised by his lack of discomfort. Had his captors healed him? Why? And how long had he been out? He needed to escape before they came back.

His semi-hard cock strained for attention and with the need to urinate. One thing at a time.

Bracing his hands on the table beside him and the platform where he'd slept, he rose to his feet. He waited for the dizziness to take over, as usual when he sat up after lying down for what seemed like forever. But it never came. All his grogginess and aches had dissipated. His limbs no longer throbbed. Had whatever they injected into his veins helped to cure his injuries?

He shuffled toward the nearest door, hands extended, ready to catch himself if he stumbled. He didn't believe he could come as close to dying as he had and not be attached to medical equipment to keep him alive. Unless he'd been unconscious for weeks, or even months. Maybe Terrans had extraordinary healing abilities his people were not aware of.

When he reached the door, he pushed it open, finding fixtures of white porcelain. A bathroom. From the images he'd studied, he found the toilet and relieved himself, thankful that part of his anatomy still worked.

Something thumped against the wall behind him. He spun around. No one else occupied the room. *Strange.* Was he about to meet the Terran who had rescued him?

"Oh, God," a woman moaned. "Harder."

English. A language he recognized. He stood up straight

and listened for more. *What kind of place is this?*

"Fuck me harder, Mare. Make me come."

He pressed his ear against the wall. His cock went rigid in anticipation. *Yep, no damage there.*

When another cry of pleasure penetrated through the wall, he spun around to find out whose voice he heard.

Creeping back into in the first room, he glanced around for another door, a way out, a path to the female receiving pleasure from somebody named Mare.

He found an opening in the wall—unnoticed earlier when he'd been in a rush to relieve himself—leading to a narrow hallway with a door at the end. Turning the handle, he rejoiced he hadn't been locked inside like a prison, and set out in search of the fucking couple. No one would have rescued him or treated his wounds if they wanted him dead. At least he hoped.

Slinking through a wider corridor, he peeked to his left and right, waiting for more noise to indicate which direction he should go.

"Oh yeah, baby. You know how to suck it." A man this time, his words coming out as a long sigh.

Cael grabbed his own dick and squeezed. He wanted to at least watch the couple before he jizzed. On his planet, sex was limited to mating couples and confined to the cubiculums at Narien Stadium. But the security posted outside hadn't stopped him from sneaking through the vents to watch the fornication.

He rushed to the right, his rod too hard to wait. The slurping, sucking, and cries of pleasure continued as he reached the entrance behind which the action took place. The door ajar, he dared a quick glimpse into the room. With a gasp, he stepped back into the hall, but could not take his eyes off the sight in front of him.

With her rounded pink ass and swollen sex folds in full view, a woman went to work sucking off a man. The musky scent of her desire wound through his nasal passages and drew him closer. She rested on her hands and knees on a platform, while the guy kneeled in front of her. But unlike any beings he had ever seen on the vids of Earth, the guy had blue skin. Not his deep, almost indigo shade, but lighter, closer to the color of the water he'd landed in. Long blond hair flowed over his shoulders, onto his muscular chest.

The man held the woman's shoulders with his webbed hands—yes, webbed hands—drawing her on and off his dick. "You have the mouth of an angel." He threw his head back and thrust faster and faster between her lips.

The sight stimulated Cael. They weren't trying to make babies; it seemed they were having sexual relations for pleasure. He yearned not only to bury his face in the wet pussy in front of him, but to taste the man's blue dick, feel it inside of him. Back on Narien, he'd crafted his own devices made from the soft, flimsy bark of the totmos plant, to experience the pleasure both men and women felt in the stadium, why they cried out during mating, but never seemed injured. And learn he had, anxious to be ready when he reached his thirtieth year and was allowed to mate. He'd turned that age a half year ago, with no one on his ship to be his partner. Would he finally have an opportunity?

When the man lowered his head again, his brilliant blue eyes flashed open, fixing on Cael.

Oh shit. But he couldn't move. He couldn't stop watching.

The man slowed his movements to long drawn out strokes, but didn't stop. "It seems our guest has finally woken up."

"And?" the woman mumbled around his cock.

"He appears healed." The man winked at him. "And from the hard-on he's sporting, very anxious to join in."

Cael stood in the doorway, no longer hiding, but hesitant to enter the room. Would the woman wish him to stay?

She swayed her ass, releasing the dick from her lips. "I

want him, too. Would you mind, Mare?"

Shoving his rod back in the woman's mouth, the man—Mare was his name—ran his webbed hands down her sides. He parted the cheeks of her ass to expose more of her pussy, smiling at Cael's shuddering breath. "It seems Tara wants you to fuck her, too. Ever been with a woman from this planet?"

"This planet, as in Earth?" What a strange situation. Sex had been the last thing he'd expected during the mission. Yet, he refused to pass up the opportunity, because he might not get another. With his ship destroyed, he couldn't return to Narien to experience procreation, and it would be years before a rescue team came for him— if one came at all—returning him well past the mating age.

"Yes, and don't try to convince me you're Terran. No one on this planet except the two of us has blue skin. Lucky for us, Tara's favorite color is blue. Now, are you willing to give her what she wants?"

Gods, yes. He nodded, anxious to get started.

Mare drew his hand across her swollen folds, the skin between his fingers rippling as he cupped her heat.

Her moan filled the room, leaving Cael weak in the knees.

"Well, get over here and give her a try," the man said. "Trust me, once you go Terran, you never go back."

Even in his feeble state, Cael scampered toward the platform. He grasped Tara's hips, but instead of shoving his dick deep into her, he leaned down for a taste. Lapping his tongue across her pink flesh, he relished the taste of her juices. Sweet, like the dimdom fruit back home. He sank deeper into her, anxious for more. She pushed her ass against his face and continued to suck off Mare.

His dick strained against the soft material draped over the love platform. He needed to experience the real sensation of fucking a woman rather than the bark of a plant. Rising to his feet, he ran his fingers across her wet heat. So warm and ready. Before he could enter her, the other man handed him a circle of latex. "Roll this on first. It's protection."

Protection? "From what?" Was her pussy filled with poisonous fluids?

The other man chuckled. "Generally from diseases, though I don't believe you have any from what I've seen. And from pregnancy. It would not be wise for Tara to give birth to a blue child. Once doctors from this planet realized the baby wasn't dead, they would whisk it away for experimentation. No child deserves that."

Cael grabbed the thin material, and gulped. So many dangers on this planet. As soon as he wore the translucent covering, he lined up the tip of his cock with her opening and plunged into her.

She moaned at his invasion. He gripped her hips, and a wave of intense pleasure rushed from his dick, all the way through his body. Being within her was nothing like the totmos. She was wetter, smoother, and her walls clenched around him in waves. *So much better.*

He drove in and out of her with blinding force. She bucked against him, urging him on. Pressure stirred in his groin. He recognized the sign of impending release. Gods, he wanted to last longer.

He pulled out and squeezed his cock, but his efforts failed. Liquid heat shot like lightning through his veins. The head of his cock swelled, and he came into the foreign covering.

"A newbie, eh?" Mare asked.

He glanced away, embarrassed by his performance. Even during mating, his people fucked all night. The couple would probably throw him out of the room.

Mare pulled out of Tara's orifice. He slid off the bed and sauntered toward him, resting his hand on Cael's shoulder. "Hey, no worries. I was the same in the beginning. Why don't you lie down for a bit, relax, and let Tara take care of you."

He couldn't respond, his attention on the massive blue

rod bobbing in front of him. The man, whatever he was, and wherever he hailed from, had been gifted with size. And he wanted the other man's dick in *his* mouth, and maybe buried in his ass.

When Mare placed his hands on Cael's chest, he expected the man to caress him, fondle his cock, not to shove him back on the platform. He flailed, preparing for a hard landing. But the platform cushioned his body, absorbing him into it. Much different from where he'd awakened.

The other man removed his protection and wiped the sweat off Tara's back. She stroked the side of Cael's face, a sultry smile playing on her luscious lips. What would they feel like sucking him off? Gods, he wanted to experience both the fine creatures he'd met, discover every position they could get into.

"How are you feeling?" She ran a hand down his chest, all the way to his still pulsating balls. "You were in rough shape."

She fondled him, and he gulped, trying to form a coherent thought. "I.... Fine, I think. Thank you for saving me."

Crawling between his legs, she shook her head. "Mare saved you. I only treated your wounds."

He glanced at the other man, ready to thank him, but Tara grabbed hold of his cock, and, licking the tip, left his mind blank.

"Oh, yeah." His eyes rolled back in his head, as she swallowed him.

She hummed, and he thrust his hips toward her. His dick pulsed, as her soft lips traveled its length. Swirling her tongue around and sucking him down her throat, she sent waves of liquid fire to his groin. He reveled in every new, electrifying sensation.

Something brushed his leg. He caught a glimpse of the other man kneeling beside Tara, stroking his massive rod. Mare inched closer, until his cock rubbed against Cael's.

"Suck us both."

Cael groaned. Seeing his dick next to the other man's, sliding in and out of Tara's orifice, left him shaking with excitement. But if Mare wanted his pole sucked, he was willing to do it, too.

"I want you up here," he said.

Tara glanced up. "Me?"

"No. *I* want to suck Mare's cock."

The man's eyes grew wide. Was he disgusted by the idea?

"This is an interesting turn of events." He pulled away from Tara and moved to straddle Cael's chest. "You want it; you got it."

Cael lifted his head to take in the light blue shaft. Opening his jaw, he sucked it in.

Mare threw his head back, and a growl rumbled from deep within.

Was he doing it right? He tried to emulate Tara's motions on his own cock, but with each swirl of her tongue, she stole more and more of his concentration. When Mare swayed above him, moaning, he figured he must be doing something the man liked. He became so engrossed in bringing the other blue guy pleasure he didn't realize Tara had stopped sucking on him until she removed the other man's dick from his mouth and kissed him. Her lips were soft, but the force with which they swept over his demanded attention. He couldn't think, couldn't stop the passion consuming him. Her kisses seemed removed from sex, more possessive, as though she claimed him.

She rolled over to his side and left him gasping, unable to see clearly. He drew in a deep breath and tried to focus. He lay there, alone, with Tara. Had he missed something? Where had the other man gone?

She draped an arm across his chest and nuzzled his neck. "What's your name?" Her breath sent shivers throughout his body, hardening his nipples—sensations he'd never experienced at the hands of others.

"Cael." He gasped, as her tongue lined the edge of his ear. Sex on Earth was more than mating. They had turned it into an art, tantalizing the entire body.

"I heard your name when I was studying astronomy in university. I think it's Latin for space. Very fitting."

He'd never known the meaning of his name. Perhaps he was destined for the mission, to crash on Earth.

"Well, *Cael*," she whispered. "I want you to fuck me and make me scream."

He grew hard all over again.

Mare returned to the room and chuckled. "You could have hopped on and gone for a ride while you were down there, Tara." He spread some liquid across his wrapped shaft.

Cael furrowed his brows. He didn't understand this couple, why they had accepted him so easily, or what the man had planned.

"I know, but I want him in the driver's seat. I want more of what he has to offer." Tara hooked her arms under his, and with a twist of her torso, rolled him on top of her.

He propped his weight on his arms, not wanting to hurt her. His cock rested between her spread legs, and he yearned to be connected to her, as she'd asked. But he was drawn, as well, to the swell of her breasts. He'd never had the chance to touch any before, the women of his planet keeping them well covered outside of mating.

Brushing his thumb across her silky skin, he gasped. He hadn't expected them to be so soft, delicate.

"Nice, aren't they?" Mare placed a hand on his shoulder, running the other along his cock, rolling a new layer of latex on him. "Go ahead and taste them."

Without hesitation, he leaned down and twirled his tongue along one of her pebbled tips. She whimpered, but he longed to elicit a stronger reaction from her, more like what he'd heard through the wall. Sucking her rosy flesh into his mouth, he arched his back and plunged his rod deep into her. She cried out, thrusting her pelvis into the air.

He regained his balance and continued his dual assault, savoring one tender peak and then the other while rolling in and out. She ran her fingers through his locks before gripping him and pulling him up. Wrapping her arms around him, she returned her lips to his and drew him into her intoxicating kiss. Even though he'd just met her, the passion she fed him with her supple lips made him feel welcome into whatever relationship these two had.

But he retreated from her as a cold liquid spilled down the crack of his ass. She pulled him down. "Relax, Cael." Her hands traveled down his spine until she grabbed his rear. Encouraging him to move faster, she moaned louder with his every drive. She slipped a finger into his asshole. In and out, then there were two, stretching him, and yet he wanted more.

Another set of hands—webbed—grabbed his hips, followed by a soft grunt. He'd temporarily forgotten about the other man. What did he have planned? Tara's fingers disappeared, but a stronger force prodded where they had been. He froze, focusing on simply breathing.

Mare's initial push stung, but Cael moaned once he began a steady, slow rhythm. "You like that?"

"Uh-huh." Gods, he hadn't expected the rush, the excitement that consumed him. Synapse after synapse exploded with fury throughout his body. Not even close to the same sensations as the toys he'd crafted on Narien.

Oblivious to the movements of the couple surrounding him, he rocked between them, finding his own rhythm. He filled one then was filled by the other. Pressure built in his loins. His shaft swelled. He couldn't think straight. Only feel the intensity. He collapsed on Tara's chest, gasping for breath. She shuddered, and her muscles gripped his cock even tighter.

Mare thrust deep into him, and he blew his load into Tara. She cried out, clenching his arms, milking him through her own orgasms.

"Fuck," Mare bellowed, his prick pulsating in Cael's ass.

He'd worried he would release prematurely, but reaching orgasm at the same time as his hosts, his rescuers, left him relieved and fulfilled. He couldn't have asked for a better place to crash land.

"Thank you for letting me be a part of this, today," he whispered.

"Today, and always, if you want," Tara said, nuzzling his jawline.

Mare pulled out of him, gone for only seconds before returning with a cloth. He ran the warm wetness over Tara, wiping away her fluids then pulled off the latex covering and cleaned Cael. When he'd finished, he left again, taking Cael with him.

They entered another bathroom. "Feel free to wash up," his host said. "I will meet you back in the room when you are finished."

With no idea how many of the fixtures worked, he wet a soft cloth in the basin and wiped down his tender genitals. Gods, if every night on Earth was like this, he never wanted to leave.

Returning to the bed, he flopped down beside Tara, enjoying her warmth. But what would happen now? Would he have the chance to become a part of what this couple shared? And where was he being kept on this planet? Was his freedom restricted to this building?

She brushed a hand across his cheekbone. "Sleep. You need it."

Mare lay down on the other side of Tara, stroking her cheek. "I love you," he whispered into her ear.

She smiled then turned to face him. "I love you, too."

Cael fought the overwhelming sense of peace. There was so much he needed to learn before he could fully relax. But all at once, his mind went blank. Unable to keep his eyes open, he succumbed to the shadows.

· · · · ✳ · · · ·

Cael stirred when rough lips brushed across his chin. Opening his eyes, he didn't know what to presume after such an unexpected turn of events. What he'd thought would be the end of his life had led to a completely erotic experience. He lay tucked against Tara's back, his arm draped across her side. Her soft sighs threatened to lull him back to sleep. Wait, who had kissed him?

The platform dipped, and he glanced behind him.

"Shh." Mare pressed a finger to his lips. "I don't want to wake her, but I must go now."

"Go?" How could he leave after everything they'd shared? Tara and Mare were together, and he'd joined in. He didn't want to come between them. They'd each had a hand in saving his life and granting him his deepest desires.

"Yes, you plunged through the surface of the lake just before I left for my weekly visit to see my girl here. She rescued me, a while back, and I thought she could help you, too."

Weekly visit? "Thank you, but…. You don't live here?" How could they have such an intense relationship if they weren't a couple?

"No, I must return to the depths. My body is only able to withstand twenty hours above the surface. Then it is essential I retreat to my underwater home to recharge. Sometimes that takes days, but it's worth it." He brushed his hand along Cael's thigh, making his cock twitch. "It's time for me to go."

He stood and followed his host out of the room. "Mare, wait."

But the man kept walking, out a door, and into the darkness, the only sounds chirping and hooting creatures. He halted. "I can tell you have questions, but we need to talk out here. Tara needs to rest."

He sat beside the man on a wooden table, the boards rough on his bare ass. Coniferous trees surrounded them, except for a path leading to a crystal blue body of water, the moon reflected on its surface. Had that been where he'd landed?

"Have you always lived on Earth? I mean, when I studied the planet, I didn't remember learning about inhabitants such as yourself."

Mare shook his head. "No. Like you, I'm from a far away planet. I was…shunned from my water world for loving the wrong woman and launched into space." He pointed down the path. "My prison pod landed at the edge of the lake. Tara found me seconds from death. She nursed me back to health in her tub."

Cael furrowed his brows. "How did she know how to help us? Does she have a whole collection of visitors from space?"

The man leaned back, laughter erupting from deep within. "No, we're the only two. She's a veterinarian, an animal doctor. Somehow she knew how to bring us back to life. She's simply amazing."

Guilt rolled through Cael's stomach. He could see the admiration the other man had for the Terran. How could he intrude on what these two had? "She is, but you're leaving her alone with me. Aren't you worried?"

"Not at all." Mare smiled, returning his hand to Cael's thigh, an inch from his dick. "I trust you will take care of her until I return, and I will have as much fun with you as I do with her."

His cock jumped at the huskiness in the other man's voice. The alien's webbed fingers surrounded his shaft, drawing the foreskin on and off his swollen peak. Instant desire burned through his veins. He longed for the man to take him again before he left.

Mare slid off the table and knelt in front of him. "It's my turn to taste you." Drawing Cael's dick down his throat, he stroked himself at the same time.

He groaned into the night air as the blue man's tongue danced around his throbbing tip. *Fuck, what an incredible night.*

If living with these two meant an eternity of sexual pleasure and being a part of the love they shared, he never wanted to leave. He weaved his fingers through Mare's golden locks, hitting the back of his throat with every thrust.

The stirring of his upcoming release began in his groin, and he pulled Mare off him. Without the chance to tell him what he wanted, the other man leaned against him.

Mare lay on top of him, their cocks rubbing against each other. He had never felt so helpless, yet excited at the same time. And when his new male lover claimed his mouth, he surrendered to the passion consuming him. Mare rocked above him, grinding their slick shafts together and bringing him closer and closer to climax.

He gripped the other man's muscled arms, unable to hold his release any longer. Mare lifted his head when Cael cried out, struggling to breathe. His body shuddered as the orgasm ripped through him.

Shifting to one side, Mare grabbed their cocks in one strong hand, and stroked them both. The tension built again. His lover's grip tightened, and with a blinding light behind his eyes, he came. Mare joined him this time, his roar silencing the creatures of the night. Their warm seed spilled together across his stomach.

The other man lay beside him, his arm heavy on his chest as he tried to catch his breath. After a few minutes, Mare rose. "Come with me and wash up. Then I must go."

As his lover headed to the water, his steps grew slower, seemed to require more effort. His color faded. Had he been away from his home too long? Gods, what would happen if he didn't get back in time?

Cael couldn't let anything happen to the man who'd saved him. He ran in front of Mare and tossed him over his shoulder. He didn't struggle.

Cael rushed into the lake, and once in up to his knees, he heaved him into the wetness. He splashed cool water over the lethargic man. *Please don't die on me.*

All at once, Mare opened his eyes. He placed a hand on Cael's chest with surprising strength. "I'm okay now." He immersed his face in the wetness then came back up. "Thank you for saving me."

Cael breathed in deep, trying to slow his racing heart. "It's the least I could do." He helped him stand, but remained in place as the other man ventured farther from shore.

He turned and smiled. "Take care of her until I return."

How could he not? She'd accepted him into her fold, unbothered by two blue men who were not from her world. He would always protect her, as much for Mare as himself.

He remained in the water until Mare dove into the dark blue depths. Then he returned to Tara's dwelling, longing to curl up against her warm body. She was all his for a few days. And when his male lover returned, their triad would be reunited.

THE DUNGEON:
A THANH ACADEMY SHORT STORY

Hunger pierced Rower's body like a thousand tiny needles digging into his skin. Food wouldn't fulfill his need. Only sex, the lust-filled cries and fragrant scent of a woman or two in the throes of ecstasy. And he had a club filled with females from all over the universe to choose from.

Staring at Kaye and the Terran female on the dance floor, he wished at least one of them would have agreed to his offer. But, no such luck. Probably for the best anyway with Kaye's fragile body and her new lover's timidness. At least he assumed they were lovers, the way they stared into each other's eyes as they ground against each other. One or both would likely freak out as soon as he started to feed, unaware of his incubus ways. The last woman he'd been with had passed out, turned into a temporary stiff right after what she claimed was "the most intense orgasm of her life".

A giggle came from behind him. Rower spun around to see Mizzie and Cynan huddled together and tapping away at Mizzie's wrist com unit. Beautiful women, yet untouchable with their air of confidence that seemed to keep others away, and their solid relationship. Though, he'd heard rumors they occasionally invited another person to join them in their sexual play. If only he could be so lucky.

A minute later, Kaye bustled toward them, her transparent exoskeleton turned a cloudy grey color, the Terran hot on her heels.

"I have to leave." Kaye ran her hands across her suit, snapping the pieces together for a tight seal. "There's a rain warning. If I don't go now, I'll be stuck here for the night. Victoria's coming with me."

Rain? Not a chance. His reptilian skin granted him the ability to sense the presence of water, predict the wet weather he avoided as well. While precipitation did lay ahead in the future forecast, it wasn't coming tonight. Had Kaye's sensors malfunctioned? "Um, are you—"

Cynan shoved him back. "Okay." She glanced past her petite friend and winked at Mizzie. "Have fun. Don't do anything I wouldn't do."

Sneaky ladies. They must have set their friend up, tapped into the program that controlled her sensors. When Kaye was out of earshot, he wrapped his arms over Mizzie and Cynan's shoulders. "What naughty friends you are, making your roommate rush out of here like that. I think you both deserve a spanking."

Cynan cupped the cloth covering his groin area, giving his balls and cock a light squeeze. "Sounds like fun. What do you think, Miz?"

The breathing apparatus on the back of the liggle's head opened and closed. A wry smile spread across her pale lips. "I'm game. It's been a while since we included someone of the male persuasion."

So the rumors were true. His cock hardened and he yearned to set it free from behind his loin cloth, feel the soft touch of the two women with him, slide it in and out of their slick pussies. If they truly meant what they said.

Rower ignored his fear of rejection and led them forward. "To the dungeon then." The less time they had to travel for a private spot, the less likely the women were to back out.

Standing before the large set of double doors at the back of the club, he stared into the retina scanner then waited for the locks to disengage. After the click, Rower opened the door on the right and allowed his lady friends to enter first.

The musky scent of sex and the moans of many engaged in the act invaded his senses. He wiped salivation from the corner of his mouth, ignoring the tingle under his skin. Swallowing his hunger, he led Cynan and Mizzie down the dimly lit hallway, neither of them pausing to gape at the scenes they passed. Many rooms were already occupied, all open to curious onlookers. In one, he spotted his friend Clarsjon, a large insectoid, fucking a female grey as if his phallus functioned like a humanoid. The woman's aura radiated throughout the space, appealing to his appetite, drawing him in to feast.

Soft fingers tugged on his hand, dragging his attention back to the women he'd invited inside the private establishment.

"So, are you going to follow through on your threat?" Mizzie leaned in close, brushing her breasts across the back of his arm. "Or should we go ahead and play without you?"

Her whispered question sent erotic visions flashing through his mind. Rower clutched both their hands and guided them to the first unoccupied private room, ignoring the tempting fragrance along the way. He closed the door behind them before leaning against it, struggling to gain control over his cravings. If he fed too soon, he'd drain the life out of the women with him.

Faux torches sent light flickering around the area, illuminating the far wall that displayed various sexual implements he could use to dole out their punishment and heighten their pleasure. An electric whip and flogger hung side by side, but he preferred the dillidium, a flat and round piece on the end of a long handle, ideal for discouraging bad behavior.

Lifting the apparatus from its hook, he grasped the handle. It had some give, allowing Rower a better grip. Taping the head to his palm, he shuddered from the bite of impact.

"So, who wants to be spanked first?" He turned away from the toys to find both women already naked. Mizzie stretched her bare torso across the restraint horse, her hands and feet already on the rests. Cynan kneeled behind her and ran her forked tongue along her girlfriend's slick folds. How had he not noticed?

Rising to her feet, Cynan ran her palms across Mizzie's ass cheeks. "She's all ready for you. Though, I'm looking forward to my spanking, too."

Lust darted through Rower's veins. If he didn't know better, he'd assume his dates were the ones looking to gorge on him. They knew exactly how to tease and torture him with their words and actions. If not for his appetite, he would drop the dillidium, whip out his cock, and fuck Mizzie hard until he burst. Then he'd do it all over again to her friend.

Tightening his grip on the device, he stepped forward. At Cynan's side, he wrapped an arm around her and drew her into him. Though he had to stand on the tips of his toes to reach her, he kissed her soft yet demanding lips, tasting her friend's desire with every ply of his tongue. Then he moved away before he became too wrapped up in pleasuring the purple-skinned vwae. Their time together would come later. Letting her go, he focused on the liggle spread out so beautifully before him.

"What are your limits, beautiful?" He yearned to fuck her until her eyes rolled back in her head. But so far, he only had permission to spank her.

"Spank me." She glanced over her shoulder and licked

her lips. "And then I want to experience what that tongue can do that your species is so famous for."

He shivered, tempted to fuck her with his tongue right then.

Cynan circled in front of him and cupped his straining cock. "And if you're really lucky, you can bang us both with this big cock of yours."

With a groan, he rocked into her fist, but before he knew it, he moved into nothing but air, Cynan's attention having returned to Mizzie.

She ran her palms over the globes of her lover's ass then along her back, raking her finger nails across Mizzie's pale skin. Such a glorious contrast between the two of them.

"Are you going to spank her or not?"

Rower shook his head, returning his thoughts to the task at hand. "Safe word?"

Mizzie lifted her ass. "Rain."

Stars, he looked forward to reddening her skin. "And yours, Cynan?"

She raised an eyebrow. "Earth. Now, let's get going."

No point in keeping them waiting any longer. He moved to Mizzie's side, planting his feet firmly on the ground. He raised his arm and with a quick flick, he slapped the dillidium across her ass.

Mizzie lurched forward on the restraint, her knuckles white from her tight grip on the planks. No sound at all until she moaned, settling her body back in position.

"You okay, Mizzie?"

"Um-hmm."

Though he couldn't see her face, he could tell she chewed on her bottom lip, perhaps waiting for his next strike. And he refused to keep her waiting. Shuffling to the left, he raised the dillidium again. *Smack!*

Mizzie's cry filled the room. But instead of shrinking away from him, she raised her ass higher. The sweet scent of her pussy filled his nostrils. He kneeled behind her and set the dillidium to the side, no longer yearning to spank her. Grabbing her hips, he used his thumbs to part her folds. As he leaned closer, he darted his tongue inside, tasting her feminine nectar. He felt her tense then relax before she rocked into him, back and forth, sighing with every movement. Lust emanated from her, catering to his hunger and ramping up his own need.

Another presence invaded her aura. Rower opened his eyes to find Cynan leaning over her girlfriend's body, staring at him. He wrinkled his forehead, too preoccupied with Mizzie's pleasure to stop.

Cynan stuck her finger in her mouth before circling it around Mizzie's asshole. The liggle's motions became frantic, her moans breathy and higher pitched. When Cynan plunged her finger inside the puckered hole, Mizzie tightened around his tongue, passion pouring from her in waves, overwhelming his senses. He fed and plunged deeper into her, gorged on her arousal until she burst with a loud shriek, pushing him out of her.

Rising to his feet, he basked in her pleasure, a dizzying sensation of desire and need.

Cynan pounced on him and knocked him off balance, shoving him back to the wall. She kissed his neck, her grip on him never wavering. "I know what you really are," she whispered in between her torture on his sensitive skin. "I want you to fuck me, feed on me until you can't take anymore."

Before he could stop her, she clicked open the belt of his loin cloth and tossed them aside. She dropped to her knees and took his dick in her mouth. Upon inviting them into the dungeon, he'd expected to feed on their desire for each other, not to have it directed as him. Stars in the galaxy, he'd lucked out with these two.

Rower thrust toward Cynan, enjoying every suck and swirl of her tongue. He caressed the short tentacles on the back of her head, losing his mind in the sensation of it all.

Mizzie joined her girlfriend in front of him, alternating

between licking his balls and Cynan's erect nipples.

Cynan released him for a moment, shoving her chest closer to Mizzie.

"That's it." He circled to the other side of them, wanting to draw the attention away from himself. They continued without him, kissing and sucking until Cynan lay atop Mizzie, ignoring his gaze. She slid down her girlfriend, running her tongue between Mizzie's breasts then along her belly until she reached between her legs.

Mizzie spread her legs and lifted her hips. Wasting no time, Cynan inserted two fingers before bending over to lick her girlfriend's clit. The liggle's aura flared again, nearly knocking him back. So much sustenance, like an all-you-can-eat dinner. Yet, Cynan's aura remained only luke warm. She seemed to gain comfort in pleasuring her girlfriend, but received little bliss of her own.

Yearning to rectify the situation, he kneeled behind her and ran his webbed fingers across her ass. He hadn't spanked her yet. Not wanting to bother with the dillidium, he decided to use his bare hand instead.

Cynan moaned with the first slap, still content to orally gratify her girlfriend. But Rower wanted a better reaction. He would make her stop what she did and focus on him, what he'd done to her, even if for two seconds.

He swatted her again, his palm stinging from the impact. Cynan lurched forward and yelled. Anger ignited throughout her aura before being replaced by a healthy dose of desire.

As she glanced over her shoulder at him, he could read the lust in her gaze. "I want you to fuck me now. Hard. No fooling around."

Nodding, he rose to his feet. "One moment." No way would he have sex with anyone unprotected. Even in the dungeon, safety remained the number one requirement. He grabbed a can from the shelf beside the implements and sprayed a thick coating all across his cock then waited for it to dry into a flexible membrane.

Returning to his position behind Cynan, he clasped her hips and ran the tip of his cock through her slick folds. She pushed back on him, allowing his cock to slip inside. A wicked invasion of his senses. Sucking in a breath, he leaned his head back. His own desires mixed with their pleasure abated his hunger tenfold. But he refused to stop, instead thrusting in and out of Cynan while she tongued her girlfriend's pussy. All he'd dreamed of and more.

Then they moved away, almost as if in a dream. Out of nowhere, Mizzie knocked him flat on his back. She climbed over him and touched her sweet lips to his before nestling onto his dick.

As she fucked his mouth, Rower clutched the globes of her ass and pounded into her. He surrendered to the fire smoldering low in his belly, let his own lust consume him.

Sensing the presence of another, he opened his eyes. Cynan smiled at him from above. "Mind if I join in?"

Sitting up, Mizzie winked at her. "Not at all." She kissed her girlfriend with such passion, Rower forgot to breathe. How they stayed so close while involving another in their sexual activity baffled him, but he had no intention to ask.

Nudging Cynan's thigh, he eased her over his face without breaking them apart. Using his tongue, he swept a path through her most tender flesh to her clit. Back and forth, enjoying the ragged gasps of the women above him. When he slid his tongue deep into her, she thrust back, taking all he had to offer. Cries of pleasure escaped between kisses as he fucked them both. Pressure built in his loins, a ship ready to launch. He tried to press on, wait until he pleasured Cynan and Mizzie. No such luck. He squeezed his eyes shut and clung to Mizzie, pumping with all his might.

Cynan suddenly froze, her thighs clenching his head. She released a throaty scream before her sticky sweetness coated his tongue.

Yet, even her release, his soul feasting on her pleasure,

couldn't hold him back. He burst like a supernova, consuming everything around him in the fiery explosion. Shrieks echoed throughout the room. He couldn't move, pleasure, lust, and satisfaction restraining him as they filled every pore of his existence. A regeneration of his soul, one he'd avoided for too long.

Several moments passed before he found the strength to move again. He glanced around for Mizzie and Cynan, to ensure he hadn't drained their life force completely. Instead of the limp bodies he'd expected, he spotted the pair snuggled together in a chair in the corner of the room. They smiled at him as if his feeding hadn't affected them.

Cynan abandoned the chair and knelt beside him, wiping her fingers across his forehead. "How are you feeling?"

"Great. Maybe a little overwhelmed." No feasting of bliss had ever left him barely able to move. But the energy coursing through him seemed supercharged, a powerful propellant for his existence.

"We're glad." Mizzie joined her girlfriend on the other side of him. "Because we've never been with another feeder before. We know how much we can take from each other, and from non-feeders, but not you."

He furrowed his brows, unsure if he'd heard the liggle correctly. "You both gorge on ecstasy, on another's release, like me?"

"Yes." Cynan helped him to his feet, her aura a radiant orange, full of passion and unwavering energy. "We've been curious about you for a long time, but we worried a moment of passion would lead to... complications."

"And now?" Sure, a feeder could be dangerous to anyone if they hadn't learned control. But he'd never gained nourishment and dispensed of it at the same time. With the two women he'd just enjoyed, he'd do it over and over, until he had nothing left to give.

Mizzie cuddled up to his side, draping his arm across her shoulders. "We want to do it again. Next weekend, only at our place instead of here at the dungeon."

"Deal." One he wouldn't refuse, their nourishment more fulfilling than anything he'd ever tasted.

The women dressed while he cleaned and straightened the room. With a wave and a smile, they departed, filling Rower's mind with erotic images of how their next encounter together would unfold.

ALIEN LOVER

*B*right red lights exploded through the sky like a fourth of July fireworks display. But there were no oohs and ahhs from the crowd, only choked gasps while Molly and the rest of the fleet stared up in horror at the disintegrating spacecraft, her fiancé inside. A scream boiled inside until it burst from her lungs, blocking out all other sound.

Diego's jet had crashed to the ground in a fiery ball and the chip implanted in his neck, reading his vital signs had flat-lined, but no traces of the chip or his body had been found. Nothing. And without that closure, Molly refused to admit he was dead.

One year ago, she'd left her role as earth liaison for the Space Service behind and set out to find him, to bring him back home. She'd abandoned family, missed holidays and birthdays, because she had to find Diego. She wouldn't go on without knowing the truth. With each passing day, despair ate away at her hope. How was she supposed to live without the man who'd stolen her heart and taken her to new heights every time they'd made love?

Slumping into her chair, she set her hands on the console, a cold sweat washing over her, and input a course for Earth. Her supplies had run low, and if one more piece of space junk hit her ship before she had a chance to repair it, the hull would breach. She'd be sucked out into space and die within minutes. A tear trickled down her face. *Maybe that would be less painful than moving on.*

No! She'd never taken the easy way out, her year of searching proof of that. She would go home and accept the inevitable; Diego had died. She would never find someone like him. No one would replace him in her heart or her bed.

She reviewed the coordinates she'd programmed. *All set.*With a heavy heart, she reached over to hit *engage.*

"Incoming message," the computer chimed. "Source located one nautical mile away, starboard."

She brushed her hands across the console and brought the video feed from the ship's right hand side onscreen. The image quivered, and she groaned when it finally became clear. A Moloxian Starcruiser.

Shit! I just want to go home. During her search, the crews of the few Moloxian scavenger ships she'd come across had been willing to let her pass if she traded with them. But she had nothing left, only enough food and fuel to reach Earth, and even then she'd be hungry during the last leg of her journey.

"Play." She decided to listen to their demands, give them what they wanted, and move on. She had no other choice. Starvation was a better alternative than providing the sexual services they'd always hinted at. The Moloxians, though humanoid, had scale-covered bodies. So incompatible with her own. She wouldn't survive unscathed and didn't sleep around anyway.

"Prepare to be boarded." The deep computerized voice shook her. No slur, and therefore not Moloxian. Who the hell was he?

She didn't have time to contemplate. Her blood boiling, she gripped the arms of her chair. The creature, whatever species he happened to be, planned to come onto *her* ship. No one boarded without her permission, which she would not grant. At the sound of her transporter, like the pitter-patter of rain on Earth, she leaped from her seat and spun around. She grasped her bolt stunner and pointed it at the figure materializing into solid form before her eyes.

With a huge outline, the male boarding her ship would only bring her trouble. If his strength matched his size, she had one option: to kill him. She took in his bare, broad chest, sculpted abs, and muscled arms. His skin shone with brilliance, as if the sun rested behind him. She gazed up at his dark hair and warm brown eyes. He studied her with an intense stare while his soft lips curved into a smile.

She gasped. "Diego?"

His smile widened. "I've been searching for you."

While she wanted to run to him, to jump into his arms, her body rebelled. She couldn't move. Her legs rubber-like, she collapsed to the floor.

Diego rushed to her side, yanking her up against him. "It's okay, *mi amor.* I've got you."

Tears flowed down her cheeks. After all this time, she'd found the man meant for her. *Just when I was about to give up.*

He kissed her forehead. "Don't cry. I'm right here. I won't leave you."

She glanced up at him. "You're not…." A sob escaped. "Dead?"

He chuckled and stroked the side of her face. "I assure you, I'm very much alive."

Trailing his fingers down her back, he inhaled, pushing his chest against her breasts. How she'd missed the feel of his firm body, the sense of security her provided. He gripped her ass and ground his erection into her stomach, igniting her desire.

Yes, very much alive and ready.

Her immediate need shoved all other emotions away. Even though their relationship revolved around love and respect, sex with Diego had proved to be an out of this world experience. And his arousal reminded her of those times, heat zinging straight to her core. "It's been so long."

He tilted her chin and leaned down to capture her mouth. With soft lips, he tasted hers, his tongue sliding between her parted lips. Gripping her ass, he lifted her. She wrapped her legs around his waist, anxious for more. His cock pressed against her core, too much material in the way for her liking. *Gods, I need him to fuck me, need confirmation that this isn't a dream. It's all too surreal.* Months had passed since he'd fucked her the night before he left. She rejected the idea of waiting to experience that union once again.

Setting her feet back onto the ground, she took matters into her own hands. With a tug, she opened his belt, followed by the button on his pants. The gravity of the ship and the weight of his gear belt bared him for her. "Still going commando, I see."

"I don't like to be restricted."

She smirked at his familiar phrase. No undergarments meant one less thing for her to remove. There would be no seduction this time. Raw need consumed her every fiber.

Wrapping her hand around his pulsing dick, she stroked up, rubbing her thumb across the tip, spreading the pooling moisture around. He rocked forward, grasping her shoulders, and moaned. How she loved that sound.

She kneeled in front of him and lapped the head then planted tender kisses up and down his shaft, her thumb trailing along the thick vein. *Fuck that.* She wanted all of it. After a quick inhale, she relaxed her throat and encased him, her lips reaching his balls.

His grip tightened. "That's it, suck my cock."

She raked her teeth back up his shaft before sucking him back in. Nothing was better than having his prick in her mouth, except maybe if it was in her pussy. She continued to draw him in and out, reveling in the control she had over him. Delighted by the pleasure she brought him, she moved faster.

"Oh, baby." His leg muscles tightened and his movements became erratic, a sure sign of his imminent release. "You do that so well."

She continued her oral play, eager to milk him dry. With a loud groan, he gripped her head and plunged in deep, spreading his seed over the back of her throat. She swallowed to torment him further. Smiling around his cock, she gained satisfaction with each jerk of his body and fulfilled grunt. But he tasted different, saltier. What had he been eating since he'd been gone?

He brought her up to him and claimed her lips. Unlike other guys she'd been with, one release always meant more with Diego.

He stroked her tongue to ecstasy, tearing off her Lycra shirt. Her breasts spilled out, nipples peaked in excitement. She clung to him, needing the contact, the reassurance that she would never again be without him.

Pulling him down to the floor, she grasped his firm rear end. She broke away, straining for breath. "Fuck me now. I don't have the patience for your teasing. You've been away far too long."

He slid down her legs, yanking her pants with him. "I don't think so. After all I went through to find you, I plan on doing this my way."

She paused. "What *did* you go through?" He'd been out there alone, for over a year.

Drawing his thumbs along her inner thighs, he shook his head. "Doesn't matter. The point is I found you. And now I'm going to enjoy my treasure."

That meant her torture. He'd take her all the way to the brink of an explosive orgasm, only to leave her hanging. Yet, when he finally granted her release, she would be clinging to the edge of sanity.

With a devious grin, he licked his lips. "Open up, baby, because I want to taste you."

Even before she spread her legs, she creamed, anxious

for his tongue to graze her clit. As he penetrated her with his thick finger, she shuddered. Two fingers and he filled her. Three fingers…*holy fuck!*

Planting her feet on the floor, she rode his digits. Harder and harder. With every plunge, he hit her G-spot, leaving her head spinning. But he stole the control from her, lifting her legs into the air and nibbling her ass cheeks to continue his torment. Pressure built deep inside her until she was aware of nothing but the fullness of her pussy and the sweet pain from his nips on her butt. One flick of his tongue against her swollen nub was all it took to end the agony. No waiting this time. She exploded with blinding fury. "Oh gods."

He continued to stroke inside her. She shuddered, riding the last waves of her release. Her body shook, whimpers escaping from deep inside.

"Baby, what's wrong?" He scooped her up in his arms and cradled her against his body.

She'd longed for such an intense release ever since he'd kissed her goodbye on the tarmac. Now that she'd found it, her mind filled with confusion. "Why…why did you take so long to find me?"

"I—" He brushed her hair off of her shoulders and kissed his way down her neck before meeting her gaze. "You were always one step ahead of me."

He'd been behind her the entire time? "But how?"

"I picked up your signal around Ginnun. Ever since, you've always been one leap, one light year away. You never rested, never stopped long enough for me to catch up, until now."

What signal? She'd been careful to keep her transmissions short and scrambled, the ship cloaked. And not once had she contacted anyone near Ginnun, the home of an emotionless race who treated visitors as trespassers. She wouldn't have dared.

Warning bells echoed through her mind. *Danger! Don't trust him.*

"Where am I from?"

He furrowed his brows. "What kind of a question is that? We're both from Earth. Molly, are you okay?"

"How did you survive the explosion, and where did you get the Moloxian Starcruiser?"

"They transported me out of the ship and held me captive. Through some lucky wagers, I gained my freedom and transportation."

Examining his features, she couldn't help but think there was something different about him. But he knew her name, had a plausible explanation. Could his desire to satisfy her and his knowledge be enough to stop her subconscious from screaming out warnings?

He circled her and pressed his cock against her ass. Her need to be fucked pushed all doubts aside. She wanted him. Now. She twisted around to straddle his waist.

Without wasting a second, he plunged deep inside her.

"Oh gods."

The man with his cock sunk into her pussy wasn't Diego. He was even bigger and thicker than the man she loved, the man she'd lost. But who was this shape-shifting being who wanted her to think he was her fiancé? Speared by his abundant prick, she stared deep into his eyes, searching for some clue.

"You're not him, are you?" Her heart clenched when he lifted her off of him and then set her into the captain's chair.

"No, I'm not." His cock now limp, he slumped his shoulders and sidled toward the transporter.

If this...creature wasn't Diego, where was her fiancé? What had happened to him?

The look-alike stepped up on the platform and turned to face her, his eyes glassy. "I'm sorry if I hurt you. When you passed me near Ginnun, I experienced all of your pain. I thought if I could be him, even for a short period of time, I could ease some of your heartache."

She stood. "But I was cloaked. No one could see me."

He didn't make sense.

"I told you, I felt your emotions. Your cloaking was the reason I couldn't find you until now."

He'd stayed on her tail all that time? "But why would you follow me for so long? And why are you taking Diego's form?"

"Diego, the one you're searching for, right?"

She nodded, biting her bottom lip to keep from revealing any more of her thoughts. Though she didn't expect to hide anything from the being in front of her.

"I'd never experienced such raw passion from anyone in the galaxy. I wanted to understand how a child of Earth could love another so much with all the fighting that has occurred for millennia on your planet."

"You're Ginnunian?"

He chuckled. "No. I sense emotions. I don't suppress them. I was in their space, taking a break, clearing my mind."

With a shuddering breath, he stood tall on the platform. "Goodbye, Molly. I'm sorry I—"

"Wait!" She refused to let him leave, not without knowing. "Diego. Did you kill him? Is that how you took his form?"

"Gods, no." He stared at her as if she'd cursed every planet in the known galaxy. "I would never harm anyone. I try to help them. Though with you, I'm not so sure I did." Glancing away, he shoved his hands behind his back.

"Then how did you know what he looked like?" Except for the size of this man's cock, she would never have known for sure, probably would have suppressed her doubt.

"Your thoughts and feelings come to me in images, and Diego was always at the forefront. I shifted to this form long before I found you. I thought his would be the best to soothe you."

A life form that cared more about her than himself? No one except her fiancé had ever put her needs above his own. But where was Diego? "Have you...felt him anywhere in space? Do you know if he's still alive?"

He shook his head. "No. If he loved you the way you do him, I would have found him in my travels. I'm sorry."

Her chest tightened. Diego really was gone. She had no one left. Her eyes burned with the onset of tears.

A gentle, yet firm hand drew up and down her back. He'd left the platform and kneeled beside her. Had he changed his mind?

"Please don't cry. I can't leave you like this."

She should be afraid, worried about the intergalactic traveler's intentions, but she couldn't deny the comfort he provided or the lust that filled her. She gazed up at the shape shifter, staring into Diego's eyes. No difference. "Don't go. Stay with me." She would rather have him return to Earth with her, in Diego's form, than to go home alone.

"I will never be him."

His breath tickled her neck, and she yearned to have him inside her again, to be filled by him.

Her fiancé or not, this man knew how to bring her pleasure and had proved he cared by following her across space. She spun into his arms, unable to let him go. "You're the closest I'll ever have. Please don't leave." Lifting up to her toes, she kissed him, hoping to convince him to stay. Still naked, she pressed against him.

His cock grew hard again, and he wrapped his arms around her. He leaned down and placed gentle kisses along her neck and shoulders. "You are the sexiest creature I've ever met. I will remain with you until you no longer need me. If you're sure."

"Yes," she moaned, desperate for more.

He scooped her into his arms, carrying her over to the bunk at the back of the ship. Laying her gently on the mattress, he sat beside her and trailed his fingers down her bare skin.

She closed her eyes and sighed. Her body tingled all

over from the ministrations of the naked stranger beside her. "Fuck me…."

Flicking her eyes open, she stared at the look-alike. She didn't know what to call him. "What *is* your name?" She couldn't address him as Diego now that she knew. But in her fiancé's form, he made the pain of her loss easier. And his present body was compatible with hers.

"Does it matter?"

"Yes." Screaming out some random name during the throes of passion would give her pause, and she didn't need that. Best to find out now.

"Ohlan. I know it is probably not a name familiar on Earth."

"It's perfect." She yanked him on top of her. "Now, take me, Ohlan."

Her loins quivered when he lay on top of her, his cock pressing between her legs. She opened to him, breathing in his musky masculine scent. This guy emulated everything correctly.

He plundered her mouth, his ravaging tongue revealing his desperation. Had it had been as long since his last sexual encounter as it had been for her? Anxious for more, she rocked underneath him, loving the pleasure his cock brought rubbing between her labia. She wanted more. He'd been inside her once, and now she yearned for the full experience.

She turned her head to the side, gasping for air. "Enough…with the…foreplay. I want you in me."

His kiss-swollen lips turned up into a smile, and his eyes twinkled. "Are you always this anxious?"

"No, but—"

He cut her words off, trailing kisses down her neck, hitting that spot right below her earlobe that made her go limp. She whimpered, her tongue numb from his torture. Never in her life had she expected sex with an alien to bring her so much pleasure.

He inched down her body, sucking a pebbled nipple

into his mouth. "Oh, fuck yes," she cried out, moisture trickling down her thigh. Extraterrestrial or not, he knew her body, teasing her most sensitive areas.

He shifted to the other breast and inserted a finger into her core. "Still so wet."

"'Cause I want you," she moaned, clenching around his digit.

He only laughed, continuing down her body. Spreading her legs open, he removed his fingers and dipped his head between her thighs. He flicked his tongue along her clitoris, sending jolts of intense pleasure throughout her body. She bucked against him, running her hands through his hair. Her pussy ached to be filled. "Yes, that's it, Ohlan."

He dragged his tongue down to her heat then probed inside. The fullness shocked her. Nothing like the pliable muscle of a tongue, but solid like a man's shaft.

Diego had no appendage like that in his mouth. Was the extraterrestrial between her legs revealing his true self? She gripped his head, encouraging him to continue. But he pulled out.

"No," she cried. "Don't stop. That felt so good."

Yellow eyes gazed up at her, no longer matching her fiancé's. "I can't keep his shape any longer." His words were strained.

"I don't care. Please, I offer myself to you." The time for doubts had come and gone. She would make it work no matter what he looked like.

He plunged his thick muscle inside her, darting it in and out. She rocked against his face, drinking in the intensity of having her G-spot licked. Ohlan's nose teased her clit, and the combination sent her to the edge and beyond. Her body tensed then released. The orgasm barreled through her in a frenzy of simultaneous explosions.

The creature swirled his tongue around her swollen folds. She struggled to hold still as the sensations continued. *Gods, he knows how to draw out pleasure.*

In an instant, he raised onto his knees, showing off his sleek figure. He reminded her of a runner, with taut muscles all over his body, his skin a deep purple.

She stared at him with admiration. Never had she met a space traveler from beyond Earth she would consider gorgeous. Not until Ohlan.

She pulled him down, tucking her leg under his, and rolled on top of him. It was her turn to explore. Trailing her fingers down his chest, she followed them with kisses, his skin soft and warm.

When she reached his shaft, she licked the head, tasting the same briny mixture she had earlier. He moaned beneath her, gripping her shoulders, his touch encouraging her. She drew him into her mouth, but he grasped her under her arms and pulled her to straddle his waist. "Enough of that. Molly, I want you to ride me."

She raised an eyebrow. "Who's the impatient one now?"

Reaching into the storage pocket over her bed, she found protection then rolled it over Ohlan's dick. She pressed her hands against his chest and raised her hips, positioning the tip of his cock between her folds. When she let go, she sank over his shaft and leaned back. The fullness she'd experienced before didn't compare to what she felt atop him. He completed her in a way no one else had. She arched her back with abandoned longing, grinding against him. "Fuck, you feel so good inside me."

"I don't want to be anywhere else." He pinched her nipples between his thumbs and forefingers. "And I have so much more to give."

Intense warmth pooled in her stomach. But she froze when something firm pressed against her anus. His hands were still on her breasts, and his cock buried deep in her pussy. "What's that?"

He gripped her waist as if afraid she would flee if he let go. "I have two…what you call penises."

Hell, yes. "How did I not notice?" She'd been down there, ready to suck him off and found only one cock. A second was something she would not have missed.

"It's not as long and remains inside until I'm close to my release."

Hells to the yeah. She'd found all her fantasies in one with Ohlan. Diego had to use a dildo to double-fuck her. This guy could do it all by himself.

After picking out another condom, she reached behind her to roll the lubricated rubber over his smaller knob. She closed her eyes and lowered onto both of his shafts. The pain from the stretch of her tight ring ebbed away as liquid fire shot through her veins. Her sighs of pleasure met Ohlan's deep moans. She gyrated back and forth, another orgasm on the horizon. He tightened his grip and rocked her faster.

The wet slap of sex echoed all around them to match the musky scent that filled the air. She was so close to climax, but held onto it, hoping to wait for her new lover.

Tucking his hands under her ass, he lifted her and thrust into both of her holes. *Yes! So full.* The power behind his movements sent her straight over the cliff. She couldn't hold on any longer.

"Fuck, Ohlan, I'm coming." Her pussy clenched tight around him, but he continued pounding into her, driving her mad. She dug her fingertips into his chest, ready to lose her sanity. A second wave of pleasure hit her, the dance of light behind her eyes, blinding.

A loud roar escaped from Ohlan, and with one final thrust, he released, his muscles pulsing inside both of her holes.

"That was galactic," he said between shallow pants.

"Agreed." Nothing she'd ever imagined could compare to the experience.

Molly shifted off him, satisfied beyond belief. She wanted to rest, but the compulsive desire to clean up first kept her from relaxing. She also kept moist cloths in her bedside pocket, and pulled two out. She wiped off Ohlan's double cocks and herself, tossing the cloths along with the used rubbers into the trash compactor then returned to her cot to lie beside her new lover.

He wrapped an arm around her, drawing her against him, his still rigid primary cock resting in the crack of her ass.

"Thank you for following me, for finding me," she whispered. Sleepiness had crept up on her, and she could barely keep her eyes open.

"You needed me." He stroked her hair, lulling her further into sleep. "And I needed you. Now rest, *mi amor*."

She smiled at the endearment and closed her eyes. Her return trip to Earth wouldn't be so depressing if Ohlan stuck around.

Molly groaned at the piercing scream of her alarm clock. She sat up and smacked the off button, gasping for breath after her erotic dream.

A manipulation of her subconscious, since Diego lay naked beside her, no purple skin or extra cock. Though wouldn't that be a treat?

The time had come for him to leave for his solo mission into space, but she hesitated to wake him. Would he really die in a blazing explosion? Was there any truth to the dream that left her heart racing?

Diego opened his eyes and smiled. "Good morning, *mi amor*."

After a deep breath, she pushed all her doubts aside. "Good morning."

He rolled on top of her and kissed her nose. "I'm so glad we were able to spend last night together without having to sneak around. At least Captain Hannigan understands that she can't stop the passion between us." He grazed his lips across her chin and down her neck. "And when I return, I'm going to marry you, Molly. You can count on it."

She hoped his words rang true, that she hadn't foreshadowed his demise. Her life would never be the same without him.

He sucked one of her nipples into his mouth, and she moaned, thrusting her hips into the air. She always wanted more. "I wish I could make love to you again, Molly, but I don't have time." He moved to the side then scrambled off the bed.

Watching him slip on his flight suit, her chest ached. Nine months would be a long time without the man she loved, but there were several new alien colonies on Earth to keep her busy. Some species adjusted to the planet without issues. Others needed a firm reminder of the seven core values.

Diego leaned down to kiss her. "I'll see you down on the tarmac in about an hour. I've got to report for mission briefing."

She waited until he'd left the room before sliding out of bed. Fear blanketed the room. The telltale twist of her gut told her the day would not end well. As much as she yearned for Diego to stay, hoped he would never leave her side, she couldn't stop him. The mission to scout new territory for the Space Service had been his dream since childhood, long before they met during their initial SS orientation.

She shuffled to the shower where her tears of trepidation burst forth. All of her crying had to happen now, before she said goodbye to Diego. He couldn't know how worried she would be while he was gone. No, she had to be brave, had to show him she would stay strong while waiting for his return. She raised her face into the spray of water, washing away the tears. *No more.* Turning off the flow, she breathed in deep and forced herself to smile. He would not see her weak.

Diego sat in the cockpit of his jet by the time she reached the tarmac. Anxious to say good-bye, she rushed toward the vessel.

He removed his helmet and beamed at her. Excitement radiated off him as she climbed the stairway. But his smile faded, the closer she came.

"Molly, what's wrong?"

A sob escaped her. *Shit*. So much for the façade. "I'm worried for you, Diego. Nobody knows what you'll encounter."

He took her hand, drawing circles along the top with his thumb. "This is what I've been trained for. I'll be fine. All I want you to worry about is picking out the perfect wedding dress."

"I know, but—"

"Come here." He drew her closer, claiming her with a sensual kiss. Hoots and hollers surrounded them, but she never wanted to leave his embrace, his touch. When he pulled away, she whimpered.

"I promise everything will be okay." His eyes flashed yellow right before he winked at her.

She gasped. Had she really seen the change in color? "Ohlan?"

He nodded. "I will always be there for you, *mi amor*. In this form or another you will always be my girl. Everything will happen as it is meant to be. I am confident you will know what to do next."

The steps pulled away from his jet, and she lurched forward. She gripped the railing, her heart hammering in her chest. "Ohlan, wait."

"I love you, Molly." He donned his helmet and waved. The shield closed over him, cutting off their connection.

Molly rushed down the still moving stairs and hopped off at the bottom. She raced over the edge of the safety line to watch him take off, pacing among the onlookers, certain of the fate of Diego's vessel.

The engine roared, generating power for the jet. Waves

of exhaust rippled underneath. She clenched her fists when the countdown began. This couldn't be the end. There had to be more. And then she noticed the purple glow amid the exhaust. Inside the jet, a helmet floated, without a body. She glanced around, but no one else had noticed.

When the countdown reached zero, the space vehicle shot forward, arching into the sky before the end of the runway. Molly glanced down at her watch and waited. One minute. Two. At five minutes, the silver speck in the sky burst into a brilliant flame.

The shocked moan of the crowd surrounded her, but she refused to be caught up in the reaction. She tore across the tarmac toward the Personal Space Vehicle, slower, but sturdier than Diego's jet. As liaison, she had the codes for the control system, so she powered up the PSV. Unlike in her dream, she wouldn't search for Diego. She set a course for neutral space around Ginnun, and would wait for Ohlan there.

A voice came over the communication system. "Power down. With the recent accident, clearance cannot be given."

A command she refused to follow, for she would never return to Earth until the love of her life was with her again. She hit *engage* then gripped the arms of the captain's chair. The jet lifted, zipping her into the sky. She would follow the love of her life anywhere. "Ohlan, I'm on my way."

LOVE IN DISGUISE

Nothing good ever happened on Valentine's Day
for Aeria. Not from the moment she opened her
eyes to hours later when she lay in bed,
contemplating her latest failed relationship. February
fourteenth of the year twenty-two, thirty-five started out
no different.

Eyes squeezed shut, Aeria waved her arms, hoping to
trigger the sensor to turn off the blasted alarm threatening
to pierce her eardrums. Lifeways always invaded their
employee's lives, telling them where to live, setting alarms
to ensure they arrived at work on time, and sending a
doctor to the home of anyone who could not go to work
due to illness. At first, she'd thought they'd cared about
her, until she'd been dumped by her boyfriend two days
earlier. Heartbroken, she couldn't bear to sit in a cubicle all
day and had an android councilor banging at her door not
ten minutes after calling in sick. Like a machine knew
anything about love and emotions. She'd answered the
bots questions, but the ache of rejection still hung around
long after the thing had left.

With the ear-splitting noise finally off, Aeria sat up and

rubbed the crusty, dried tears from under her eyes. Her chest ached from the sobs that had wracked her body for most of the night as she'd tried to sleep. She had no will to go into work again, but dreaded another visit from robo-councilor.

After programming her replicator to brew a pot of coffee, she headed to the bathroom for a pee and a shower. Aeria turned on the faucets and the pipes clanged. Only a small trickle of water dripped out of the showerhead. One would think with all of the modern technology in the apartment building, the pipes would have been replaced long ago. But no, Lifeways thought it nostalgic, a way to honor an era. And she would have to go without a shower, again. Using the slight amount of water she could manage, Aeria wet a cloth and used it to wipe away the sweat and ick of the previous day from her body.

She glanced into the mirror, remembering the morning Shaun had come up behind her at the sink, kissed her neck and down her back, gotten her begging for sex before he'd at last carried her to bed and took her. Where had things gone wrong? They'd talked all the time, went on dates, and had an enviable sex life. Then, out of the blue, he'd told her their relationship wasn't what he wanted anymore, that he was moving out and transferring to another city.

Her chest tightened. A tear escaped. Then a sob. Crying once more. She couldn't help herself. She'd loved him, thought they would be together forever. How was she supposed to go into work in the cubicle next to where Shaun had worked, remember all of their stolen glances, whispered words, and even their private moments when everyone else on the floor had left for the day. She couldn't. Not today. Maybe not ever.

Through tear-blurred eyes, she left the bathroom and glanced around the apartment for her communicator. She couldn't go into work. The pain was still too fresh.

Finding the device on her end table, she called the

human resources department. She swallowed the lump in her throat and explained to the computer on the other end why she wouldn't be in her cubicle in an hour.

Without dressing, Aeria returned to her bed. The android from Lifeways could waltz right into her room for all she cared. It wouldn't be bothered by her nudity, probably wouldn't even notice. She drew the covers over her head and tried to push away the images of Shaun flooding her mind.

Knock, knock, knock. "Aeria?"

She woke with a start. Somehow, she'd fallen asleep while waiting for the robo-councillor. But, it wasn't the android. It was a woman's voice, more organic than anything she'd ever heard from a robot. Had she dreamed it?

"Hello?"

"Good morning, Aeria. I'm Dr. Lafleur, but you can call me Sophie. May I come in?"

She saw the woman's silhouette in the doorway. Definitely not a machine, but she had to work for Lifeways if she possessed a key card to get into her apartment. "Yes, just give me a moment to put on a robe."

Since when had the corporation stopped using robots to make personal visits? Aeria didn't know they still had professional humans working for them. All people she'd ever seen were used as mindless drones in cubicles—like her—feeding information into the computers and answering tech calls when the automated service failed to answer an inquiry.

"Lights forty percent." She grabbed her robe off the back of the nearby chair and wrapped it around her body. No need to give the doctor a show. She didn't want to end up in the hospital due to a broken heart. She needed time.

When Aeria exited the room, she saw the doctor had already seated herself in the chair, her long black hair flowing over the back. Aeria walked over to the couch, anxious to begin their session. Talking to an actual person might make the pain more bearable.

"Can I get you something to drink?"

Sophie shook her head. "No need, but thank you for the offer.

Aeria sat down, pulling the lower part of her robe over her legs to ensure she didn't reveal too much. She glanced up, taking in the doctor with her knee-length tweed skirt and pale pink blouse, clothes of a previous era, they showed off her feminine beauty, her perfect porcelain skin. She was everything Aeria wanted to be, and yet never had the chance, not when born into the working sector.

Then she caught a glimpse of a pulsing blue light on the side of the doctor's neck. A microchip. It had to be.

Aeria sucked in a deep breath and stilled, not sure what to make of the woman in front of her. Sophie looked every bit as human as her. Yet, the microchip common to all Lifeways androids shined bright, an unmistakable glow.

"You're a robot?" She winced, worried she might offend the doctor if she was human.

Sophie blinked and folded her hands in her lap. "I prefer the term artificial intelligence, but yes, I am."

"But how? You look real. If it weren't for the chip...." Aeria rubbed her own neck. "I never would have guessed."

"I am a model thirty-nine dash seventeen. Though we are all referred to by our given names." She crossed her legs and pulled down her skirt. "Human resources believed I would be their best resort in helping you get back to work."

Of course. They were only concerned about keeping their employees at work. "So, you're going to ask me questions and hope that makes everything better, just like the android they sent yesterday?"

"No." Sophie shook her head. "I am moving in. I have been dispatched by Lifeways to live with you."

Aeria scrunched her face. "Live with me? For how long?"

"Forever." She smiled, the twinkle in her eyes

unnaturally human.

"Why?" Was this Lifeways way of preventing her from ever dating another man? No guy would want to come back to her apartment, let alone reside with her, knowing the corporation had another hold on her life. Having an android was a death sentence for one's social life, a way of putting her on house arrest. Work and home, nothing more.

"I do not know. I only know my instructions, and those are to punish you and pleasure you."

"Wait! What?" Aeria leaned back in her chair, away from the woman who looked all too excited about punishing her. "I haven't committed a crime."

"Missing two days because of another person is unacceptable. I am here to prove to you that you do not need a man in your life."

She cocked her head to the side, confused. "But I like men. Why couldn't Lifeways have sent a male android?"

"Your psychological analysis and past history indicate I am the better choice." The doctor reached into the bag she had set on the floor, and pulled out a wooden spoon. "Now, come over here."

Aeria didn't move. "What are you going to do with that?" Make her cook? She didn't have any appliances—those were a luxury—just a replicator.

"I am going to hit it across your bare bottom as your punishment." She tapped her thighs with her hands. "Now, come lay across my lap."

Aeria crossed her arms, staring at the woman. "No."

The doctor raised her eyebrows, a far too human reaction for an android. "If you do not follow my orders, the guards outside your door with come in and escort you to the hospital. Now, which would you prefer?"

Ice filled her veins. Not the hospital, never in a million years. Once a person from the working sector went in there, they never came out. There were rumors Lifeways used them for experimental treatments. Some even claimed they'd looked through the windows of the building and seen people strung from the ceiling like puppets. Aeria had never gone close enough to find out, and she didn't plan to.

"Fine." She stood and made her way over to the woman. A spoon across her ass was a safer penalty. Using the coffee table for support, she kneeled down and laid across her thighs. They were warm, as if blood pumped through her, not at all what she'd expected from the android. "I will accept my punishment."

"Good." Sophie rolled up the hem of Aeria's robe, exposing her rump to the cool air. She rubbed her cheeks with her bare hands. Warm again. "Now, I will give you five spankings for each day of work missed."

Aeria gulped. "Okay. Please be gentle."

A smack filled the room a millisecond before a swarm of bees stung Aeria's ass. She yelped and jerked off the android's lap. Not gentle at all. Not even close.

Sophie grabbed the belt of her robe and pulled Aeria back into position. "You must hold still. If you do not, I will call the guards. This is the punishment you chose, and you must accept it."

Aeria didn't respond, instead focused on her breathing, willing the pain away.

The second spanking came without warning, too, this time to her other cheek. She dug her fingernails into her palms, the sting worse.

"Better." The doctor massaged the skin she had just smacked. "You are getting the hang of this."

Sure, but how was a spanking supposed to cure her broken heart? The memories of Shaun remained fresh in her mind. She couldn't just set them free.

Whap!

Aeria screamed. Electric shock traveled from her raw skin to the very tips of her body. Tears ran down her face. "Stop, please stop."

"That is only three. I still have seven more to give

you."

"No." She wouldn't be able to handle it. "Can we save them for another day? You're living with me forever, right? Isn't that punishment enough?"

"I am afraid I cannot *save them for another day*."

The doctor hit her again, and a fifth time. Aeria cried out with each one, blinded by the pain and tears.

Sophie rubbed her ass again. "You are doing well. Five more to go."

Aeria tensed, waiting for the next unexpected strike. It never came. She relaxed, but only a little, under the doctors soft hands.

Smack!

Sophie's bare hand this time, the spoon gone. Aeria whimpered, ashamed at being caught off guard. The pain radiated up and down her spine.

The last four came hard and fast. She'd barely had time to catch her breath in between each one. Her bare skin burned, her nerve endings lighting up with sparks in a rhythmic dance, the sting never fading.

Her sentence over, she pushed off the doctor's lap, but Sophie held her down.

"You have received your punishment, and now I will bring you pleasure."

"How?" The thought escaped her lips. Androids weren't made to provide gratification. They lacked the knowledge and desires.

"By stimulating you sexually." The doctor slipped her finger between Aeria's ass cheeks and along her vaginal folds.

Aeria jumped. "Wait. I... I'm not into women. Or robots."

"Your profile indicates otherwise." Sophie helped her to her feet. She untied her robe and slipped it off her shoulders, letting it fall to the floor.

Out of fear of the guards outside her door, Aeria whimpered. She didn't want a machine to pleasure her.

Yet, the hospital was a much worse alternative.

The doctor slid off her own skirt and unbuttoned her blouse, no undergarments below."Shall we do this here or on your bed?"

Aeria blinked hard. A female android wanted to have sex with her? Why? Because she'd taken two days off work after her boyfriend had dumped her? She had to be dreaming a crazy, messed-up fantasy. Yes, it had to be. If not for the cool breeze across her still burning ass, she'd believe it, too.

"Um...." Aeria tried not to notice the woman's perky tits, the way they pointed up at the tips instead of being round and smooth like her own. And the doctor had no pubic hair. If she did grow hair there, she'd been recently waxed.

Aeria groaned. She wanted to see more, touch the woman in front of her, find out just how real Lifeways had made her. Not in a sexual way, no, that wasn't possible. She was simply curious. Nothing more.

Sophie reached out and ran her fingers down Aeria's arm. "Why don't we go to your bedroom?"

She gasped, frightened by the sudden lust she felt at the woman's touch. Turning away, she shuffled to her room, trying to imagine Shaun's naked body, any of the guys she'd been with. But she couldn't picture any of them, only the naked female android who followed right behind her. Her heart raced. Was the doctor right? Was she meant to be with a woman? Was that why none of her relationships ever worked out?

Aeria paused at the food of the bed, unsure what to do next. Her inhibitions had fled on the way to her room, but she dared not initiate anything. Not for her first time.

Sophie met her from behind, her breasts pressing into Aeria's back, her hip bones to Aeria's ass. The sting of her spankings seemed to have been chased away by her sudden desire. The doctor brushed her fingers along Aeria's breasts, down her sides, all the way to the creases of her legs. She moaned as Sophie kissed the back of her neck, her lips soft and warm.

In a heartbeat, the doctor spun her around and caressed her body.

Desire shot through her like a raging fire. She'd never wanted anyone more. Yet, she had no idea what to do with a woman, how to find pleasure and give it in return. Had Sophie been programmed with such knowledge?

The doctor kissed her lips, forceful, yet gentle at the same time. Warm and inviting. Aeria opened to her, their tongues mating in a seduction dance. She grasped Sophie's hips, pulling her closer, never wanting to let her go. Android or not, the woman drove her mad with lust. Unexpected and out of the blue, but she felt right being in her arms, like she'd finally found what she'd been looking for all along.

Aeria leaned back onto the bed, needing it's support before she melted into a puddle of ecstasy. Sophie followed, her body seeming to be in sync with Aeria.

Sophie seated herself between Aeria's legs, running her hands along her stomach, all the way up to her breasts. Aeria took in a deep breath, her senses clouded. But the doctor, the android pushed on, circling her nipples, tugging at the erect peaks. Sophie leaned down and sucked on them, her tongue swirling over the sensitive flesh.

Thrusting her hips in the air, Aeria wanted more. She ran her fingers through the woman's hair, panting hard.

Sophie reached between her legs, parted her folds and slipped a finger inside. Aeria gripped the sheets, the thrill more intense than she'd expected. The doctor rocked over her, matching pace with her strokes. Another digit entered her. Then a third. Full. Yes, full and loving it.

Aeria pulled Sophie up her body, craving her kisses, and a way to pleasure her. If possible for an android to find release. She became lost in the passion, all her wants, needs and desires fulfilled by a machine, one far more advanced than any she'd ever come upon. One differentiated into being so very female. No cock, but the doctor worked her body with what she had.

Aeria's hunger grew, pleasure pooling low in her belly. A muffled cry escaped her lips.

Sophie rained kisses down her neck, leaving her gasping for air. Her strokes became harder and faster, using her palm to brush Aeria's clitoris.

Aeria clung to the bed, her release agonizingly close. Every muscle wound tight, she burned with passion. In a frenzy of carnality, she burst, shockwaves rippling through her. She held Sophie tight while her body convulsed. When her grip loosened, the doctor moved, straddling her thigh. Sophie ground against her. Was she seeking out her own pleasure?

Aeria wrapped her other leg around the woman and stuck out her tongue, reaching for a taste of the firm breasts bouncing above her. A slight whimper from the doctor and she wanted to do it again. This time, she sucked the nipple into her mouth, flicking the tip with her tongue. Sophie moved faster, the motion giving Aeria a new buildup of pleasure.

Lost in the motions, Aeria felt nothing but Sophie. The rubbing and strangled cries of the woman left her delirious.

Sophie jerked up, throwing her head back. She shuddered above her, releasing a high-pitch moan. Her erratic movements set fire to Aeria's own release and they rode each other's thighs until the sensations died down.

Sophie lied down beside her, a wide smile gracing her pretty face. Aeria beamed back, still struggling to catch her breath.

"Well?" The doctor raised her eyebrows.

"That was... amazing." Aeria turned to face her new lover, the one who would be living with her forever. "Hard to believe you're an android."

Sophie release a deep breath. "I, um, have a confession to make."

Aeria sat up, unsure what the woman had to say. Would she end up at the hospital anyway?

The doctor reached for her neck and pulled off the microchip. "I'm not an android. Heck, I'm not even a doctor."

Aeria scuttled back on her bed. "What? Who are you?"

"Someone who has admired you forever." The woman inched closer, reaching out her hand. "Aeria, I work two cubicles over from you, but you've never noticed me. All these guys you date walk all over you, take what they want and then leave. Yet, you can never see it."

"You have no right!" As mad as she was, Aeria glanced away, shame trumping all other emotions. She knew the people who worked around her, didn't she?

"I knew Shaun had left and when I didn't see you for a second day at work, I decided to try and help."

"So you spanked me?" She shook her head, still trying to process the truth. "You deceived me."

Sophie winced. "I did."

"So, you're not a doctor or an android from Lifeways? There's no guards waiting to take me to the hospital?"

The woman shook her head. "I'm sorry, but I was trying to make you see what you were missing. My name *is* Sophie Lafleur. That much is true." She rose from the bed, appearing less confident than she had when she'd arrived. "I'll see you at work tomorrow."

"You're not leaving." Aeria left the bed and blocked the woman's way out. "There's no way. First of all, you deserve some spankings of your own for deceiving me. And second, you said you would stay with me forever. You may have lied about the other stuff, but I'm holding you to those words."

"Really?" A smile crept across Sophie's face.

"Yes." For once she wasn't alone on Valentine's Day, and if Aeria had her way, she would never be by herself again.

THE POWER OF THREE

Oscar groaned as Delayna rubbed her husband's ass, her signature move in seducing him. Even though Bo feigned sleep, the man's twitching foot gave him away. Next, she would reach around to grasp his cock, and Oscar held his breath in anticipation of the move.

As her hand rode up Bo's shaft, Oscar closed his eyes, imagining her fingers tightening ever so gently on *him*. Just enough to amplify his need. She dragged her thumb up the vein on the underside of his dick. *Oh yeah*. And then back down. *If only….*

He didn't have to worry about going hard; the body he occupied was already made of stone.

The gargoyle statues around Delayna's house and yard provided several bodies for him to occupy. He moved in spirit from figure to figure, watching her every day, hoping to eventually feel her touch, and Bo's, too. He watched from the headboard tonight, waiting for the day he'd finally be set free.

She didn't waste any time with foreplay. No, she'd already fingered herself to orgasm before involving her husband. Even with her small frame, she managed to flip Bo onto his back. She draped her leg across him, straddling his waist, and then eased with a sigh onto his fully engorged dick. Swaying her hips, she ground against him.

"That's it, Del. Ride me like a fuckin' cowboy."

Oh, to be in Bo's place. But tasting, savoring both of them would be even better. He yearned to stick his dick in someone's empty mouth or ass. Flesh slapped against flesh. The musky scent of sex wafted into his nostrils, as if he was home with his own lovers.

Shit! Even though he remained as stone, desire rushed through what was left of him, centering in his non-existent groin. He craved a real body so he could stroke himself, get off somehow, and release all his sexual frustration, built up since he'd been cursed to this form, to this place.

Delayna rode Bo harder and harder, making the headboard shake. The banging inched Oscar closer to the edge. The heart he no longer possessed sped up. What would happen if he fell off, broke? Would he return to his world, or would his life be over?

His stone feet teetered on the edge.

"Oh, God, Bo, I'm so close."

He wanted to revel in her upcoming orgasm, to imagine her pussy squeezing his tool, but he worried too much about his own end. With one final thrust, the headboard slammed the wall and he tumbled off, hitting Bo's forehead with a thwack then fell to the ground.

Fuck!

Bo hollered, shoved Delayna off him then grabbed Oscar from the floor. "Goddammit. Now I'm going to have a goose egg from a fuckin' gargoyle."

Climbing off the bed, she reached for Oscar, but Bo held him high in the air, out of her reach.

"I'm so sorry. Give him here, please."

A mix of emotions washed across her face, ending with a frown. Was she worried about him or Bo? She reached up for him again, rubbing her sweaty, naked body against her husband's bare chest.

Oscar forgot his predicament. He longed to be pressed between them, sucking on her perky tits or groping Bo's big rod. *Just a little lower.*

"Listen, Del. I understand your obsession with the paranormal, but does this thing really need to be in the bedroom?"

Oscar's heart raced, the man's fingers achingly close to his stone cock. He needed out of the statue. *Now.*

"I don't complain about the model airplanes all over the house, including this spaceship looking one that's suspended above our bed, do I?" Stepping back, she settled her hands on her hips.

The view? Perfection.

"That Stealth Bomber is worth more than your silly statues and doesn't cause concussions."

She rolled her eyes and lunged, making her tits bounce. "Really, because I could've sworn you hit your head on it the other day when we were making the bed. Now, give him here, please."

"You don't care that this *thing* hurt me, do you?"

"Maybe he's jealous that you were getting some and he wasn't."

Ain't that the truth.

Bo glared at her. "So not funny."

Did she know he was really in there? Could she feel him watching her, wanting her?

Bo lowered him to her palm, but didn't let go. "You and your creatures."

She leaned forward and kissed the bump on his head, her breast rubbing across Oscar. "But you love me anyway."

A loud crack filled the air. Light surrounded Oscar and he was falling.

As if being sucked out of the stone, he sprang from his prison and landed on the floor on hands and knees. Taking a deep, refreshing breath, he stood and stretched his arms high into the air in all his naked glory. Being confined to such a small space had left him stiff, and not in a good way.

Delayna gasped, glancing from him to the broken bits of stone on the carpet.

"What the hell?" Bo grabbed the bed sheet and draped it over his wife, knocking the gargoyle remnants in her hand onto the carpet. "Who the fuck are you, and how did you get here?"

He stumbled back. "I'm Oscar and I think, somehow, you both set me free." The evil sorceress, Catalis, hadn't bothered to explain how the curse worked, tossing him into this world and the stone figure before he'd had the chance to ask.

Delayna giggled as she eyed him from head to toe, her gaze sending electric sparks along his spine.

He winked at her. Now that he could move, he longed even more to touch every graceful curve.

Bo grabbed a phone. "I'm calling the cops."

"No," Oscar said as Delayna wrestled for the device. "Please, give me a chance to explain." Bringing law enforcement into the situation would find him hauled off to jail as an intruder. He would never cause them any harm, his simple needs being pleasure and a way home.

"Yes, Bo, let him explain."

When she returned her gaze to him, he noticed her resemblance to his Lianna on Wigbay. He'd never seen Delayna so close, on the same scale. The women shared the same dark, captivating eyes and full, kissable lips. Their breasts perky, plump, and a perfect fit for his large hands. Is that why Catalis had sent him there—to torture him with a woman who looked like his female mate? Bo reminded him of Lewis a bit, too. His heart and cock pulsed, and he yearned for his lovers and the couple before him.

"Fine. Explain to me why we have a strange man in our

bedroom, with a hard-on that freaks me out since he's staring at *me*." Bo snatched a pillow and held it in front of him, blocking Oscar's view. Even though Bo seemed uncomfortable with attention from another man, his dick seemed to have a mind of its own. Oscar could work with basic desire. It made him ache to experience this couple even more.

"I'm from Wigbay," he stated. "I'm not sure how to explain where that is except to say, it's in another dimension. I was sent here, trapped as a spirit inside your gargoyle statues when I refused to take on another female lover."

On the day he'd been sucked away from his life partners, Catalis had arrived at his shared home, shouting curses and calling him out for not taking her as his mate. Against their advice, he left Lianna and Lewis on the love platform, anxious to dispose of their unwelcome visitor. But she had other ideas.

When he met her outdoors, she waved her arms in wide circles, uttering an ancient chant. Her malicious words drew the air around them into a swirling mass. Without the combined power of his mates, he was weak to stop her. Catalis used an energy field to bind him then tossed him into the center of the twister. Lianna and Lewis raced out the door and launched themselves onto the sorceress, but they were too late.

"You were in our statues?"

Oscar blinked hard, returning his attention to his hosts.

Bo's eyes grew wide, his face a mess of contradictory emotions.

"Another lover?" Delayna asked.

"I've been able to move amongst the gargoyles you own for the past year. It feels like forever since I've seen Lianna and Lewis—my mates, my lovers." A wave of sorrow threatened to wash over him, but one glimpse of the sparkle in her eyes brought back his immediate need.

"You've been spying on us for a year?" Bo turned to

his wife. "I don't believe this shit about being trapped, but there could be hidden cameras in your statues. Microphones. There could be people across the planet who've listened to our conversations, watched us have sex. I swear, Delayna. I'm throwing every single one of them away as soon as we get this whackjob out of the house."

"Please, Bo." She whispered something in his ear and he smiled until he caught Oscar looking at him.

Bo stood up, letting the pillow fall to the floor. "Like what you see?"

He smiled, taking in the man's full figure, each rippled muscle, his thick arms, legs, and luscious cock. "Oh, yeah."

Delayna giggled again, tossing the sheet aside. She spun around as if eager for him to see all *she* had to offer.

Yet he already knew and was anxious to sample. *Oh, to be sandwiched between these two.*

Bo scowled, but his betraying shaft stood up even straighter. "So, what the hell do we do now? How do we get you back to wherever-the-fuck you're from?"

An idea formed in his mind, one that would leave him satisfied in so many ways. These two had set him free from his prison of stone gargoyles. Perhaps they could send him back to his sanctuary as well? "A ménage? It was your combined touch that unleashed me in the first place."

Bo's face turned red. With clenched fists, he stepped closer, his nostrils flared. "Get. Out."

Delayna squeezed between them. If only they could move that position to the bed, against a wall, anywhere.

"Maybe…if he just watches…?" She chewed on her bottom lip, making him yearn for a taste. If her flavor matched her scent, he would sample cherries with every lap of his tongue. *Gods, let's get started.*

Bo grabbed her shoulders. "You believe him?"

She nodded. "He appeared out of nowhere. You saw it, too."

Glancing down at the crumbled statue, Bo sighed.

"It might be exciting to have someone watch us. You

88

always like to try new things." She stroked his dick then moved to the side, waving Oscar closer. "And maybe you could teach him some of your stellar moves."

Oscar had been watching long enough to know *all* the man's moves. He wanted to experience them for himself, sample every inch of their bodies, but saying so would most likely halt Bo's evident arousal.

Dropping to her knees, Delayna took her husband's cock into her mouth.

Oscar moaned, imagining her moist lips circling his own dick. Bo grabbed her hair, thrusting in and out of her mouth. She sucked hard, taking him all the way to his balls. *That-a-girl.*

Oscar turned his attention to her rounded backside, wanting to spear her still juicy hole with his straining cock, but would the other man appreciate that yet? Was he ready for a ménage?

Standing up, she nudged her husband onto the bed then crawled on top of him. Oscar groaned, watching the sway of her hips, his erection painful.

She tumbled to the side.

"No. There's no way you're exposing your ass to him. I want to see what he's doing at all times."

She spun around, rising onto all fours to face Oscar. "Does this work for you?"

Oscar caught her sly grin along with her wink. *Oh, she's a naughty one.*

"Much better." Bo rammed into her from behind, grasping her hips and grinding his body against hers with incessant rhythm, as if showing off his prowess.

Oscar grasped his dick and stroked himself, eager to get off. The man did have moves. Yet, as much as he enjoyed watching them fuck, he yearned to be involved.

Delayna lifted a hand off the bed and crooked a finger at him, licking her lips. With two strides, he stood facing her. If she was willing, he wouldn't refuse. She grabbed his shaft and drew him past her lips. His knees grew weak; it had been too long since he'd been inside anyone's sweet mouth.

She sucked him into her moist heat until he hit the back of her throat. Then she swallowed him deeper.

Oh gods!

Bo's thrusts along with her motions brought him within seconds of release, the muscles in his thighs tight. Until her husband stopped.

"No. I can't do this. I can't watch this."

She released Oscar's dick and glanced over her shoulder. "You're so much harder than usual. Admit it, you like to watch."

"I do, but it's something more. You're *my* wife. *Mine.*" Bo glared at him.

"Then what do we do now?" she asked.

Oscar sighed. He understood, couldn't imagine sharing his lovers with anyone outside the three of them, but he had to return. If there was a way. "Just like when you freed me from the statue, I'd like to be between you. To be in the middle of your fucking might send me back. Please, I beg you, can we at least try?"

She raised her eyebrows, staring at her husband. "It's up to you. I'm fine either way."

The man muttered under his breath, leaving Oscar with a fist of worry clutching his stomach. Would he ever get to rejoin his lovers? What would happen to him if he didn't? Besides the two people in front of him, there was nothing for him in this world. He wanted to leave as much as Bo wanted him gone.

"Is this your fantasy?" Bo asked, staring at his wife. "Do you want to call it in now?"

She nodded. "But you have to be willing. I don't want to make you do it. I'm sure we can figure out another way."

Oscar remained silent, anxious to find out his fate. He could think of no other option.

"Fine," Bo said. "I'm willing, but like a few years ago

when you fulfilled my fantasy, there are some ground rules."

Oscar didn't care. As much as he would enjoy sex with the couple, he simply wanted to return to Wigbay.

Bo fixed his glare on him. "One, if you hurt my wife in any way, I *will* kill you.

Two, no one will touch my ass. It is off limits. And like before, Delayna, no pictures, video recordings, or talking about this after tonight. This is a one-time thing. If this doesn't send you back, you're gone anyway, agreed?"

He nodded, waiting for someone to make a move. Their house, their terms.

Delayna crawled across the bed to her nightstand. She pulled out a box of condoms and a bottle of lube. "We're going to need these." She then shuffled to the end of the bed, pulling him and Bo to stand before her.

Gazing up at them, she grabbed a cock with each hand. Oscar shivered in anticipation. A year of imaginings paled in comparison to the real thing. She drew Bo's dick into her mouth first. He'd anticipated as much. She had to play favorites, but he didn't.

He clasped Bo's jaw and claimed his mouth. The man surprised him by responding to the kiss rather than pulling away. He lined the firm lips with his tongue, seeking entrance. He intended to pleasure them both. When granted access, he plundered the man's mouth, taking all he offered.

"Holy fuck, that is so hot."

They broke apart to see Delayna staring up at them.

Bo pulled her into his arms. "Maybe I've had this fantasy, too."

Together, they rained kisses up and down the sides of her body, savoring every inch. Oscar edged slowly around to her front to taste more. He gently sucked her breasts, swirling his tongue around her tits. But she wouldn't have that. She fell to her knees, encasing his dick with her magical mouth. So warm. Not giving Bo a chance to object, he leaned over Delayna and took in the man's erect rod. It didn't take long for Bo to grasp his head and thrust deep inside. His thighs tightened as if he was ready, but Oscar stared up at him and squeezed his sack to prevent him from coming. *Not yet, big boy.*

The man backed away and laid his wife on the bed, then met his gaze. "I want to see you lick her cunt. And if I'm satisfied, I'll suck that big prick of yours."

He shuddered at the thought. Bo was more into the ménage than he'd expected. Oscar dove between her legs, eager to eat her sex-swollen pussy. With his first lick, she arched, grinding against his face. He plunged deeper, sampling her sweet honey. *Gods, she even tastes like Lianna.*

He easily slid two fingers inside, thrusting into her wet heat while flicking her clit with his tongue. Releasing a throaty moan, she writhed under him. "Oh, Oscar. Yeah, that's it."

"She's happy, and so am I." Bo slipped under Oscar's hips and clutched his rod. Wet lips glided over the head and down his shaft. Waves of pleasure shot straight to his brain. The man had a wild tongue.

He gyrated into Bo's mouth, while bringing the man's wife closer and closer to orgasm. Her muscles gripped his digits. And as he nipped her clit, she cried out in release. Her warm nectar coated his fingers. Her body twitched, and she sank into the bed.

Focusing his attention on Bo, he pivoted over his body to sixty-nine him. With hands resting on the edge of the bed, he sank his mouth over the cock bobbing against his face. He plunged onto the other man, breathing in the musky scent of sex and Bo's sweaty dick, until Delayna cleared her throat. As much as he hated to stop, Oscar sat up to find out what she wanted. For she'd made this all possible.

She grabbed their rods, wearing a devious smile. "I want you to fuck me. Both of you. If this is my chance to live out my fantasy, I'm going to do it right."

Oh, he couldn't have asked for a better place to wind up cursed.

Bo climbed to the top of the bed and lay spread eagled. "Climb aboard, honey. He can have the back end."

Oscar shivered with excitement. His heart hammered against his ribs. Once positioned, she passed him a condom and lube, her eyes filled with pure ecstasy. "Be gentle."

And he would. He couldn't enjoy sex unless his partners did as well. His greatest pleasure came from ensuring theirs. He leaned down to lick and nip her ass, enjoying her squeals. But with the opportunity to be deep inside her, he didn't want to waste time. Spreading the liquid between her ass cheeks, he gently slid a finger into her puckered hole. She moaned in response, pushing back against him. If he'd known her body more intimately, he'd have plunged right in, but he needed to ensure she could handle him first. Inserting a second finger, he circled them inside to stretch her muscles wide enough for him to fit.

"Now," she growled. "I want your huge cock in my ass, now."

Not wanting to keep her waiting, he sheathed his dick with latex and slicked it with lube. Ready to experience her tightness, he pressed the tip of his rod against her puckered hole. His balls rested against Bo's.

The constriction of her muscles eased as he slid into her. He'd seen her fucked in the ass before, but worried whether she'd stretch wide enough to accommodate him. The couple kept their sex life exciting, constantly trying new positions, toys, and even light bondage. Including another person was a new step for them, and he was glad to be part of the experience.

He rode her slowly, enjoying the friction from Bo's cock. Pressure built inside him from top to bottom, like a fuse ignited and waiting to explode. But as much as the sex thrilled him, he didn't want the release. He wanted to return to his lovers.

He pulled out of her. "I'd like to be in the middle, the position we were in when you freed me from the statue. There has to be a way to send me home—and if just being held between you broke me out of the statue, this seems like a possibility."

But Delayna continued to ride her husband, lying against his chest. She threw her head back, her mouth wide open, close to her release. He couldn't leave her like that. She'd been willing to help him the entire time, and he had to aid her now. He slid back into her, reaching around to caress her breasts. He kissed her satin-smooth neck and down her back.

Suddenly she sat upright, knocking him back and crying out as she came. He helped to draw out her orgasm, plunging in opposite Bo. When he pulled out, she shuddered. Moving to lie beside Bo, her breathing remained ragged. Yet she smiled at Oscar. "That was...amazing."

"I agree," he said, shifting off the bed. He retreated to the bathroom to shed his condom and grab a warm, wet cloth. He returned to clean her off. "Can you handle more? If not, just say so. I don't want to hurt you."

She nodded, a wicked grin across her lips.

He tossed the cloth into the hamper and slid between the two of them, capturing her lips while stroking Bo's shaft. She moaned into his mouth, her fingers sliding down to her pussy.

He stopped their journey. Anxious to play in her sweet juices again, he leaned down between her thighs and lapped her cunt. He plunged his tongue deeper. Her wet heat pulsed around him in time with the little whimpers from the back of her throat. Red-faced, her expression tensed, until she came undone, her cry filling the room.

A hand traveled down his shaft, and squeezed the head. Bo's. "Let's get you back to Wigbay."

He hoped Bo would sheath him, but the man simply handed him another foil package as he put on his own protection. "You sure you can handle me?"

Bo was almost as big as Oscar, but so was Lewis. "I look forward to it."

Delayna lay on the bed, smiling up at him.

He leaned down to capture her beautiful, swollen mouth. Her tongue found his and he reveled in the way she controlled him. Gasping for air, he pulled away. He rested his head on her shoulder. "Thank you for this. I will never forget either of you."

And then he entered her with a driving thrust, swaying in and out of her pulsating core. Bo lubed his ass as he rocked against the man's wife. A finger probed, and he shuddered as the tip slid past his tight ring, neglected for so long. He was desperate to have something bigger, harder, buried deep inside. His balls nearly returned to stone, heavy, aching for release, but gods, he wanted to go home and the sooner they got down to business, the sooner he'd be back with the two people he loved. A second digit. Tight, but not what he needed. He glanced over his shoulder, not wanting to waste any more time. "No, I want *you* deep inside me. Send me back, please."

The man, gripping the flesh of his ass, didn't need any further pleading. With a sharp penetration, Bo sank into him, pushing him farther into Delayna.

She sucked in a quick breath, her muscles squeezing him. "Wow."

Bo pressed down on him to meet her upward thrusts, never missing a beat. Oscar's climax built fast, starting in his thighs, as Bo's cock swelled and her pussy tightened around his shaft.

In a lightning bolt of fulfillment for all of them, Oscar's muscles tensed then filled with a tingling sensation. Slowly, he slipped away.

"Goodbye, Oscar," Delayna called.

But he couldn't respond. He disappeared into a thick haze, catching a glimpse of the couple, making love as if he'd never been there. They had given him a way to return, and for that he would always be grateful.

Closing his eyes, he waited to be reunited with his lovers. For no one could compare to Lianna and Lewis in bringing him pleasure.

A warm, familiar breeze surrounded him. But instead of his lovers, he found Catalis asleep on the platform. *No.*

With measured steps, he backed away from her, taking in the rest of the room. A metal cage hung in the corner, Lianna and Lewis curled together inside. They stared at him with wide eyes.

He placed a finger to his lips, and they nodded. Careful not to wake the sorceress, he crept over to them. Searching his memory, he chanted a spell he'd learned from the forbidden books he'd found stashed at the bottom of his mother's trunk of magical resources. He thanked the gods the former sorceress had kept that one token of her old life after she changed her evil ways upon meeting his father. And he'd inherited the genes to make the magic happen.

His lovers gasped as he whispered the dark words. But the counter-spell worked, and he lifted them out of their prison.

As much as he wanted to hold them, make love until the sun set several times over, he still had to dispose of the sorceress.

"Binding spell," he shouted.

Catalis flicked her eyes open as the three of them raised their arms and wrapped the electric current around her. "You can't have returned," she screeched, struggling against the unseen ropes. "That's impossible."

No, not impossible. "It's amazing what the power of three can accomplish." He would never attempt to handle any problem without Lianna and Lewis again. He turned to them. "We need to take her outside." He planned to make her experience the torture she'd inflicted upon him and more.

With an invisible force, they carried her out the door

and down to the shore of the lake near their dwelling. Oscar recited the forbidden words she'd used to curse him, sending her body and spirit into a palm-sized rock. Her shrieks and curses did not deter him. Stepping forward, he held the rock above his head then launched it far out into the water.

Lianna joined him at the shore, clasping his hand. "I've missed you."

He gazed into her beautiful eyes. "And I, you."

Lewis appeared on the other side. He ran his fingers down Oscar's torso, filling him with a new desire. "Let us show you how much."

As Lewis leaned down and swallowed his rod, Lianna claimed his mouth. He moaned in ecstasy, happy to be with them again.

PHOENIX SPANKED

Lucinda swiped the match, setting it ablaze. As she brought the fire to the wick of the red candle, she stared into Tavo's eager gaze.

"You're sure this will work?" He drummed his fingers across the table, offering a smile that quickly faded.

She nodded, confident the Alpha of the local wolf pack would soon be paired with the love of his life. Not from the spell they were about to perform, though. No, she had already arranged for his mate, Denise, to "run into" Tavo at the grocery store the next day. The two could not be more perfect for each other. Almost as much as she and Marta. Tavo only needed the assistance of the spell she was about to cast to give him the confidence he needed to ask the tiger shifter to dinner. Not what one would expect of someone so respected in the community, yet no one but Lucinda knew how much his mate intimidated him. And with a heavy dose of courage, he could be Alpha around Denise, too.

Once the wick flared, Lucinda shook the match free of its flame. She reached across the tablecloth, joining hands with her client. "Now, repeat after me—"

A breeze swept across Lucinda's face. The flapping of heavy wings surrounded her, scattering her collection of herbs and spell books across the floor. The candlelight flickered and died.

"In the name of the Mother Goddess." She stood and faced the source of the commotion, her wife. A phoenix with golden feathers covering her magnificent wings. "How many times have I told you not to fly through the house?"

Marta folded her wings behind her and stared at the floor, her dusty-rose hair falling over her beautiful face. "I'm sorry. It's just.... My time is coming, and you know how antsy I get right before." She dug the pointed toe of her heeled black boot into the floor. "I forgot."

Lucinda stepped forward and tucked her wife's hair behind her ear. Yes, she knew. With every change, she'd been present. She cupped Marta's cheek, smiling when her wife met her gaze. No way could she truly be mad, especially when she fought to resist the appeal of her full lips, now in a pout. All frustration faded, replaced by raging desire. Cupping the back of her head, she slipped her fingers into Marta's hair and kissed her, enjoying the quick gasp in response. Sliding between her parted mouth, she swept inside and claimed her lover. Heat balled low in her belly and her head buzzed with unending lust. Every thrust of her tongue drew moans of pleasure and kept her seeking more.

Lucinda gripped her lover's hips, drawing her closer. A growl emanated from behind, and she spun around, drawing in a long-needed breath.

Tavo stared at them with deep-brown eyes. Dark, shaggy hair covered his arms and face where they had been bare only moments before. Pointed canines stuck out over his bottom lip. "Why do you torture me?"

"Sorry, Tavo. I couldn't help myself." Around Marta, she had little to no control over her passion, regardless of her intentions.

"Why can't you just let me be a part of what you two have? There's enough of me for you both."

Marta giggled behind her. "Because you don't have the parts we like."

"And you already have a mate, anyway." Lucinda gave him a pointed stare. "You just need to claim her."

His fangs retracted, and the hair withdrew. "Well, then, let's get this spell over with."

Lucinda faced her wife. "Go to our room, and we'll discuss what happened when I'm finished."

Marta dropped her hands to her sides. "You forgive me?"

"I'll always forgive you." How could she not? The woman was the best person ever to come into her life; gave her confidence to be the witch the Mother and Father had meant her to be. "But don't think for one moment you won't receive punishment." Somehow, her lover had to learn to remain calm before her change.

When Marta slumped off, Lucinda returned to the table. She relit the candle and joined hands with Tavo. "You ready?"

The shifter nodded. "Please give me the courage to claim my mate."

···· ✳ ····

Marta paced naked at the foot of the bed. She couldn't relax. Not with her impending spanking or the fire rolling through her veins. Her changes occurred more often, once a month since she'd married Lucinda, but she had yet to gain control over them. If not for her wife by her side during every one, she would have likely set the entire town ablaze.

The door opened, and her lover stepped inside. Gone was the long, black robe she wore when casting spells. Instead, she wore a black, thigh-length fishnet dress over her purple and black tiger-striped bra and thong, the same colors as her hair. Pink gloss coated her luscious lips, but the black eyeliner highlighted her dominance. Marta focused on the sexy sway of her hips as she drew nearer, ignoring the oak paddle hairbrush in her hand.

"You know you're not supposed to fly in the house." Lucinda smacked the paddle onto her palm, not reacting to the sting, as if it didn't hurt at all.

But Marta knew the truth, and it would soon be her ass on the receiving end of those slaps. She'd disobeyed an agreement made a year ago, when they'd moved into their new house. Now, she had to accept the consequences.

As Lucinda sat on the edge of the bed, her dress rose up her thighs. Marta licked her lips. If only she could skip her spanking to run her hands along her lover's exposed flesh, part her legs, and taste her sweet juices.

Marta sighed. If she didn't accept her punishment, she wouldn't receive the pleasure that always followed. She kneeled on the floor before lying across Lucinda's lap. "I'm ready to accept the consequences of my actions."

"Good." Lucinda's husky voice sent shivers down her spine, a temporary reprieve from the flaring heat since the onset of her change. If her wife didn't hurry, she'd burst into flames before she was properly spanked.

"Five spanks, this time." Lucinda rubbed her ass. "You deserve more for interrupting my session with Tavo, but I'm willing to show some leniency due to your state of mind."

"Thank you." She sucked in a deep breath, awaiting the first smack.

Instead, Lucinda tortured her, running a finger between her swollen lips, along her clit. "Count them."

Marta cried out, gripping the sheets hanging over the side of the bed. She didn't dare object, as her wife would surely add to her punishment.

Smack!

Her body jerked as the sting sliced through her left ass cheek. She swallowed the pain. "One." Lucinda had caught her off guard with the first spanking, but she wouldn't with the next.

Inhale. Exhale.

The paddle bit into her flesh on the other side with the second spank. A whimper escaped before she had the chance to stop the sound. Perspiration ran down her forehead. The fire inside flared. "Two."

"You're doing well." Lucinda caressed her burning skin, soothing some of the pain. "You're controlling the change well. But I fear we don't have much time."

The last three swats came quick and hard. She cried out with each one, not having time to count in between. Her eyes stung at the brine from her tears. But as quickly as they formed, they evaporated in a puff of steam. Her time was coming.

Pushing off Lucinda's lap, she rose to her feet. Lucinda had doled out her punishment, and now Marta had to get to safety. All lust and desire that normally followed a spanking session fled as panic took hold. She didn't have time to grab any clothes—they'd likely burn up anyway—instead, heading straight for the door.

"Where do you think you're going?"

Marta paused at her lover's authoritative tone. "To the safe room. It's time."

"No." Lucinda held out her hand. "Come here. Stay with me."

As much as she desired to be in her wife's arms when the change took place, she couldn't risk her being any closer than on the other side of the safe room door. "You know I can't." Her fingers sizzled before blue flames burst from the tips. "I've got to lock myself away. I don't want to hurt you."

Lucinda clutched her wrist, pulling her toward the bed. "I've been doing some research, and I don't think it's possible for you to hurt me."

Marta wasn't so sure. She couldn't afford to take the risk. "Luce, please."

"Trust me." Lucinda held onto her hands, intertwining

their fingers. She didn't seem at all bothered by the flames. "I want you to lie on the bed."

Hoping her wife knew what she was doing, Marta did as told. Steamy sweat rose from every pore, the fire spreading beneath her skin. "I don't know how much longer I can hold it in." She prayed to the Mother and Father she didn't set fire to the entire house and her lover in the process.

Lucinda crawled over Marta. "You can let it go any time." She ran a finger between her wife's breasts, down past her belly button, until she found her throbbing clitoris.

Marta shouldn't have to hide in a steel box every time she went through the change. If Lucinda's plan worked, her lover would never set foot in the safe room again. If it didn't, they'd have to rebuild their house. But she trusted all the information she'd found, and remained confident neither of them would be harmed.

Circling her thumb across her lover's hyper-sensitive bundle of nerves, she reveled in every one of Marta's cries and moans. "Oh, honey, just let it go."

Her wife gripped the sheets beneath her. "I can't." She bent her knees, digging her heels into the mattress.

No way would Lucinda give up. She continued her ministrations, slipping two fingers inside Marta's slippery hold. "Trust me." She stroked her lover's cheek with her other hand, wanting to reassure her somehow. "It'll be okay."

Marta's movements became erratic. She pounded on the mattress with closed fists and shook her head. With an ear-piercing screech, she shot up, knocking Lucinda back. Her wings shot out behind her, each tip touching a side of the room. Blue flames rose through the pores of her skin, covering her entire body. The fire spread to the walls and danced across the ceiling.

A bubble of panic rose to Lucinda's throat. She was trapped. No way out. But with one glance at the tears flowing down Marta's cheeks, she swallowed her fears. She needed to be the strong one, the confident one. This had been her idea in the first place.

Focusing on her love for her phoenix, she smiled and reached into the blue flame to wipe away Marta's tears.

As quick as the fire had appeared, it retracted, not leaving any evidence of its existence. Marta gasped. Her wings and all of her hair disappeared, falling into a pile of ashes onto the sheets. She curled into a ball in the center of the bed, perspiration covering her body.

Lucinda grabbed a dry blanket from the chest at the foot of the bed. She wrapped it around Marta and drew her onto her lap. Holding her tight, she kissed her lover's bald head. Never again would she allow her wife to lock herself away during her change. They would experience each one together, until the end of time.

LAST MINUTE CUSTOMERS

Mandy handed the bag of costumes to her old high school math teacher and his wife with a smile. "Bye, Mr. and Mrs. Sullivan. Have fun at your party."

After they left, she glanced at her watch. Ten minutes until closing time, then she planned to go home and crash on her bed rather than attend one of the multitude of Halloween parties her friends and older customers had invited her to. Tomorrow, costumes had to be marked down and the Christmas and other holiday decorations brought out. Store sales from October had more than quadrupled from last year, but tonight she'd celebrate by catching up on her sleep. In the morning, on top of everything else, she had to place an ad in the paper to find more staff.

She slipped out from behind the counter to straighten the costume aisle after little kids had decimated her neat display only hours ago. She'd been so swamped, she hadn't had the chance to reorganize it again.

The door chimed. She glanced up, stifling a groan over the last minute shoppers. But the sight of the two men walking in left her unable to do anything but stare. One was tall, broad, and dark, while the other was blond and built like a track star—long lean, and all muscle. They couldn't be more opposite, yet both made her heart pound. She'd seen them around town before, but had always been afraid to engage in an actual conversation with them. What did she have to offer anyway? All of her time was dedicated to her party supply store.

The taller of the two raised an eyebrow. "Sorry to bother you when you're about to close, but we're looking for costumes, and well…. We haven't had much luck."

He was good-looking *and* well mannered? She didn't see that combination very often. Most males she considered drop-dead gorgeous knew they were hot and made sure everyone they encountered knew it, too. His mother taught him well. She stood and brushed her hands down the front of her starship commander's dress, hoping she didn't look like too much of a geek in front of him.

The blond ran a hand through his thick, wavy hair. "I doubt she's going to have anything left, Zane. No one does on Halloween night. We should have started looking before today."

"No!" She covered her mouth. She hadn't meant to yell. They stared, as if waiting for her to continue, and she lowered her hands. "I'm sure I can help you find what you're looking for. And I'll give you fifty percent off." *Shit, that sounded desperate for a sale.* Really, she wanted to keep them in the store a little bit longer. They would make excellent heroes in her future fantasies.

Zane chuckled. "Sure, let's see what you've got. My brother and I are going to a sci-fi themed party. Do you have anything that falls under that description?"

Brothers? Could have fooled her. But she wasn't about to argue. And they were into sci-fi, like her. "Sure. We have your movie costumes. Star Wars, Star Trek, Avatar…."

He shook his head. "I don't know. What do you think,

Blaze?"

"Those have been done," the other brother said. "Anything else?"

She gave them a quick glance over to gauge their sizes. Her cheeks warmed as she caught sight of the bulge in Zane's pants. A wave of desire swept over her. She inhaled deeply. They were only customers and hadn't given any indication they wanted more than costumes.

It had been so long since she'd even seen a man's cock, dedicating all of her time to the store. She needed to get out and live again. She needed to get laid.

With a sigh, she spun around. Best not to think of that now. She had customers to serve. Two very hot guys who wouldn't want anything to do with her. Men didn't notice plain women like her. It was a fact of life. Her life, anyway.

She approached the rack of large men's costumes. The men were at least that size, and she had quite a few left. Males didn't dress up as much as they wanted their woman to dress up for them. Yet in her extremely short dress, she didn't seem to attract the attention of one single male.

Plucking a couple of the expensive Transformers costumes off the rack, she held them out to the two men. "What do you think of these?"

Zane rubbed his chin. "I don't think so. Too many parts." He started rifling through the selections and motioned to his brother. "Help me look."

Mandy rushed over to the door and locked it. It was closing time anyway, and she wanted to devote all of her attention to the hot customers already in the store. If she got to know them better, she wouldn't be afraid to talk to them at the grocery store. And maybe, just maybe, one of the guys would ask her out. *In my dreams.*

A hand clamped on her shoulder. She screamed and spun around to face two aliens. Or Zane and Blaze dressed as extraterrestrial warriors.

"Holy shit, you scared me." Her heart had never beat so fast.

Blaze wrapped his arm around her and drew her into his side. "Sorry, honey, but it was pretty funny."

Honey? Did he actually mean her? "Found something you like?"

"We saw something we liked as soon as we entered the store," Zane said, reaching for her hand. He placed his lips on her knuckles then flipped her hand over and kissed her wrist all the way up to the inside of her elbow.

Her nipples pebbled against her dress. *What the hell was going on?* As much as she'd love to know what it was like to experience either of these men dressed up as aliens—or not dressed as aliens for that matter—even both at the same time—they were strangers. She had to get to know a guy before jumping in the sack with him. Though the images of writhing, naked bodies running through her mind, of what it would be like to have a ménage, left her weak in the knees.

She straightened her shoulders and tucked away those thoughts. Best not to get ahead of herself or hope for the impossible. "Mind telling me what's going on?"

Blaze pulled her closer, whispering in her ear. "We want you. But first, tell us your name."

She froze. She didn't know these two aside from seeing them on the streets and in the grocery store. What did they really want with her? Would they hurt her? Or worse? "It's, um…. M-Mandy, but…you're kidding with me, right?"

"No kidding," Zane said, suddenly behind her. He set his hand on her waist, and held himself against her. "Ever been with two guys before?"

His hard cock pressed through both their clothing to rest in the crack of her ass. She whimpered. Oh God, they were serious. She actually had the chance to live out her favorite fantasy, one she recreated often by using her toys before she went to sleep. One she never thought possible.

She spun away from him, her cheeks burning. "No, but I don't think it's a good idea."

"Why not?" Zane asked, though he backed away. "Do

you have a boyfriend? A husband?"

She shook her head. "No. It's just...." She yearned for Zane to be behind her again, to feel his warmth, his dick. *Holy shit, I really do want this.* "I'm scared."

Blaze brushed his hand along her cheek. "We won't hurt you. We just want to bring you pleasure. I can already smell your arousal."

She squeezed her thighs together. Was it that obvious?

He leaned in and joined his lips to hers. With gentle prodding, he deepened the kiss. She moaned into his mouth, desire zinging through her body.

Zane moved behind her again, caressing her breasts as he laid kisses along the back of her neck. Her toes curled. Enjoying their touch was so wrong, but she couldn't find the words to object. All doubt flitted away as primal need took over.

Blaze fingered the hem of her skirt. He lifted it and ran his hands along her thighs. So gentle. Backing away, he and Zane raised the dress up and over her head then tossed it to the floor. They caressed her body with their large hands and warm, moist tongues. *Fuck, it's actually happening!* Two men had come into her store, seduced her, and would take her. Right in front of the window.

She pushed Blaze away. "Not here. Not for everyone to see." Although some adults would appreciate the view, she wasn't an exhibitionist and didn't need the local newspaper splashing naked pictures of her onto the front page like a tabloid.

But where to take these two? The back room provided little comfort, but did she trust them enough to take them upstairs to her loft? She rubbed her hands down her arms. If she didn't decide soon, she'd need their two bodies just to thaw her out.

"Do either of you have condoms?"

Zane wrapped his cloak around her, holding her in his arms. "We don't, but I can go get some if you want."

That solves it. She had some in her bedroom. They'd

been a gift from her friends when she moved in. She'd never had any reason to test them out. Until now. "Upstairs. I have some there."

"Sounds good." He scooped her into his arms, his cape covering enough of her to go outside. "Which way?"

"Straight down this row." She gripped his neck, excitement buzzing through her. "There's a door to the left. Stairs are just outside. I live in the loft above the store." The shop door would lock behind them.

With her in his arms, Zane bounded out the door and up the metal steps, Blaze close behind them. She fumbled to enter the code to her lock and they all burst through the doorway. Zane shuffled his way around her furniture then laid her down on her bed. How he found it in the dim light, she had no idea.

Warm hands glided across her skin, lighting up every single nerve ending. Her boots were removed. Then her panties. She moaned, overwhelmed by sensation. She couldn't tell which brother lay where, but they were naked on either side of her. Their eager cocks pressed against her thighs. One brother guided her chin until she faced him. *Zane.*

He pressed his lips to hers and plundered her mouth, his tongue sweeping inside. She groaned into his kiss, hungry for more. His brother sucked on her nipple, heightening her arousal. *Holy shit.* She was actually having a ménage with two hot brothers. She thrust her hips off the bed, desperate to be fucked.

Zane slipped a hand between her thighs, drawing along her mons. But she wanted him closer, inside her. He skimmed his fingers between the lips of her pussy, filling her with charged tension. She cried out, turning away from him. "Yes, that's so good."

He drifted down to the foot of the bed, spreading her legs open. And Blaze inched farther up, capturing her mouth. His tongue tangled with hers in an erotic dance. From one man to another, they left her breathless, unable to think clearly.

Zane laved her pussy, his skilled tongue grazing along her folds, pressing against her clit. She squealed, gripping the sheets. She hadn't expected the intense pressure of impending orgasm when both men had yet to penetrate her.

"Where are those condoms?" Blaze whispered.

A new rush of desire rocketed through her veins. The guys were actually going to fuck her. She swallowed, hesitant yet anxious for the ménage to escalate. "The nightstand right beside you. Top drawer."

How was this going to work? Would they take her at the same time? Take turns? She'd never been with two men at the same time before. Would she be able to handle them?

Zane plunged his fingers into her sex. She bucked against him, her head spinning. Going without intercourse for so long had turned her wanton the moment it was offered. She couldn't wait to feel their cocks inside her.

He circled her swollen clit while gliding his fingers in and out. She quivered, the pressure building inside her. If he kept up his assault, she'd orgasm before being fucked by either one.

"That's it, honey. You're so close. I can feel it." Zane quickened his motions. "Come for me, Mandy."

He withdrew his fingers and slid them down to her anus, circling her tight hole. She writhed against the pressure of the new torment. Blaze returned beside her, sucking and massaging her breasts. Together, the men made her feel desirable.

In a frenzy of simultaneous explosions, she cried out, gripping the bed. Her release swept over her in intense waves. Neither man let up, prolonging her pleasure until the orgasm finally subsided.

Closing her eyes, she lay back, panting. It had been way too long since her last fuck. And she whimpered for more.

The brothers spread out beside her. She reached out to

grab their velvet cocks. *Holy shit!* Their dicks would be a challenge to fit inside her because of their girth. But she'd try. She didn't want to stop.

Zane leaned over her, capturing her mouth. She tasted herself on his lips, enjoying the decadent flavor. Proof he had just given her the best orgasm of her life.

Behind her, Blaze fingered her pussy, her asshole, spreading lube all over. He must have found it in her drawer along with the condoms.

Something ripped open behind her. Blaze kissed her shoulder then whispered. "Are you okay, Mandy? You still want to do this?"

She chewed her bottom lip and nodded. *Might as well live out my fantasy. Who knows if I'll get another chance.*

Zane stroked the side of her face. "This is all about your pleasure. If you experience any pain, tell us, and we'll stop. Okay?"

"Okay," she whispered. Before tonight, she never would have thought guys could be as concerned about her pleasure as they were their own.

Blaze buried himself inside her pussy. She moaned with every long, slow stroke. Zane left the bed, but his brother cradled her into him, holding her, teasing her. Never before had she felt cared for during sex.

Another condom package ripped open. Zane lay in front of her as his brother pulled out. He rolled her on top of him, his erection pressing against her heat. She'd missed the feeling of a cock filling her and eased onto him, taking him deep inside. She gasped as her pussy clenched around his shaft. Need cascaded through her body. How had she gotten so lucky?

Sitting up, she rocked her hips across his groin. He grasped her waist and quickened her movements, hitting her G-spot with every thrust. *Shit.* She lost control, could no longer hang on, her next release drawing near.

Blaze reached around her to caress her breasts. He worked them in his hands and pinched her sensitive nipples. Nibbling the back of her neck, he sent her over the edge. She bucked against his brother, riding Zane along with the waves of pleasure.

Collapsing against his chest, she fought for oxygen, struggling to calm her pounding heart. She'd just experienced the best sex ever.

Zane brushed her hair away from her face. "Are you ready for more? Do you think you can handle both of us?"

"I…." She hesitated, still scared to delve into this new territory. Except for the extra male, she hadn't experienced anything unfamiliar. Okay, so the orgasms were out of this world. But to have both inside her…? "Be gentle, okay?"

Blaze massaged the cheeks of her ass, bringing her a sense of calm in the electrified situation. "Always. If it hurts, just say so."

"'Kay." Sucking in a lungful of air, she swayed over Zane. Warm moisture dripped down the crack of her ass. Blaze massaged the ring of muscle at her entrance then slipped a finger inside. "Easy now. Relax."

She concentrated on Zane, his lustful smile barely visible in the dim moonlight shining through her windows. God, why hadn't they approached her sooner? All this time she'd wanted an experience like this, and they'd been in the same town.

The bed jiggled as Blaze settled behind her. A new force pressed against her ass. Bigger. Harder. Steadying her breathing, she tried to ignore the sharp pinch of Blaze's intrusion. He took his time, pushing in little by little, allowing her time to adjust.

With a deep grunt, he pressed his hips against her ass. "How are you doing, Mandy?"

"Good." *Oh yes. So full.* She moved against them both, taking their cocks inside her at the same time. So much pressure. Pleasure. Intoxicating fulfillment.

She burst in an explosion of ecstasy, gripping Zane's shoulders as she cried out. "Oh. My. God."

The brothers took control, driving into her until they,

too, released.

She lay, spent, on Zane's chest, as Blaze wiped her off. If she died at that moment, she would die happy. Zane wrapped an arm around her and kissed her forehead. "Thank you for trusting us."

She smiled, some of her focus returning. "My pleasure." Literally. She would never settle for the mediocre lovers she'd had in the past. From now on, it was all or nothing. And these brothers had given her everything.

Blaze lay beside her, draping his own possessive arm across her back. "Ours, too. Hopefully we can do it again."

"Yes," she sighed. Exhausted, she closed her eyes, snuggling into the crook of Zane's neck. After tonight, Halloween would never be the same.

····✳····

"Excuse me, Miss. Hello?"

Mandy flicked her eyes open and gasped. She'd fallen asleep at the counter.

Zane stared at her. Not the Zane who'd brought her unbelievable pleasure along with his brother, but the customer. It had all been a dream.

"Are you okay?" he asked.

She rubbed her eyes. "Yeah, sorry. I must have dozed off. Did you find what you were looking for?"

"We're the ones who are sorry. We kept you here late." He set his costumes down and laid his hands on the counter. "It's Mandy, right?"

She nodded, still trying to shake away the drowsiness.

"Well, Mandy." He leaned forward. "We haven't quite found everything we're looking for."

"No?" she squeaked out. She couldn't help but stare at his lips, remembering how he had used them to bring her so much pleasure in her fantasy.

"Uh-uh. See, Blaze and I are going to a party tonight and we don't have a date."

His brother approached the counter. "And we were hoping you'd be our date. Our costumes go together, like the perfect threesome."

Her pussy clenched at the thought and her cheeks warmed. A date with both of them? She squeezed her thighs together.

"That is, if you're not too tired," Zane added.

A rush of adrenaline flooded her body, washing away all of her fatigue. "I…I'd love to. I just have to close up the store."

"Great!" Blaze grinned like a kid in a candy store. "Anything we can do to help?"

She shook her head. "No, it's okay. I'll ring you through then meet you outside in a few. Okay?"

"You just made my night." Placing his hand on hers, Zane brushed his thumb over her skin. "Though I'm hoping it gets even better."

He winked, sending a shiver down her spine. Would her fantasy come true tonight? Only one way to find out. She hurried through her closing procedures, anxious to join Blaze and Zane outside.

After grabbing her jacket, she locked up the store. In the parking lot, the two customers from her most erotic fantasy waited for her. And if tonight was anything like her dream, it would be the best night of her life.

SEXY SUITORS FROM SPACE

Chapter One

Some vacation. Nothing but snow for miles. I might as well have been visiting the North Pole with all the layers of clothing I had on. And, somehow, the cold wind still managed to find the small amount of face I didn't have covered, stinging the skin around my eyes.

"Are we almost there?" I could barely see five feet in front of me, only the mountain of a man directly ahead. If he slowed down for one second, I'd grab his coat with one hand and cover the rest of my face with my free arm. But if I didn't keep up, I'd get lost in the blizzard. "Seriously, is the place I'm staying anywhere nearby?" Every other hotel I'd stayed at had the check-in desk within the building. Apparently not this one.

The man didn't respond, kept walking, guiding me, hopefully, to the glass igloo where my grandmother held a timeshare.

"Get away for a few days, Heather," she'd said, handing me the plane ticket to Finland and shoving me out the door. "You'll have a lot of fun and forget about your scum of a cheating fiancé. It's been a year since you kicked him out. Time to move on. Show off your new curves."

Sure, curves that I'd gained from spending a week eating nothing but ice cream. Not only had I gained ten pounds, but I'd started crying Ben & Jerry's. It still hadn't helped my pain. I'd loved Todd and wanted to spend the rest of my life with him. Unfortunately, my love hadn't been returned. But, a trip wouldn't make me forget what I'd walked in on two days before Christmas.

I'd tried to return the tickets. "Snow and cold really aren't my thing, Grandma." Give me a tropical beach somewhere with tanned, muscled men, and I'd at least try to get over Todd.

Refusing to take them back, she'd only patted my hands. "You'll be surprised how much fun it is in Lapland. I would go, but I'm getting too old to enjoy the...amenities. It's your turn now." She winked and shut the door behind her.

And there I was, trekking through the knee-deep snow north of the Arctic Circle, dreading the blanket of white and cold I expected to last my entire vacation.

As if a brick wall had jumped in front of me, I smacked into something solid. My guide. He'd finally stopped. If not for all of the extra layers I wore, the collision would have left a few bruises.

"We're here." He fiddled with some contraption—I assumed the lock—while I peeled myself off him.

I peeked around him to get a view of my accommodations for the next week. *Shit!* A real glass igloo, not some extravagant hotel with a dome-shaped glass roof that *looked* like an igloo. *Last time I ever trust Grandma to know what's best for me.* The woman might have raised me, but she was so out of touch with what I needed as an adult.

Opening the door, the man grabbed me under the armpits to pluck me from the snow and ushered me inside the igloo, a space no bigger than my kitchen. This was where I'd be trapped, alone, for one week with nothing to do but remember the night I'd walked into my house to find my fiancé fucking some floozy. And Todd hadn't even bothered to hide the fact he lived with another woman from her. If he hadn't raced out of the house, I swear I would have cut his balls off.

"Would you fancy me to return this evening to escort you to dinner? It will be served at six."

I spun around, my guide's baritone voice warming me from the inside out. He'd barely spoken more than two words since we'd met. He stood closer than expected, and I nearly slammed into him again, wobbling in my boots. Gripping my arms, he steadied me.

"Um...." All ability to breathe and speak flew out the door. I stared into his crystal-blue eyes, surprised by the stranger yet again. He'd removed his scarf and hood, revealing Thor-like features. My clit pulsed, alive for the first time in months. The doppelganger of the only superhero who'd ever turned me on stood less than a foot away, holding my upper arms. I'd give anything to run my hands through his wavy blond hair, kiss along the firm jaw covered with golden stubble, nip at his full lips.

Fuck being the good girl. That had only left me with a broken heart. This was my vacation, and I planned to have some fun, get what *I* wanted. A sexcation. I'd deal with reality when I returned home.

I sighed as my inner vixen decided to come out and play. "I'd much rather keep you here. We can warm each other up." And I couldn't blame the vixen. Who'd want to let this hunk go?

Todd who?

Thor dropped his hands and smiled, but the upturn of his lips didn't travel all the way to his eyes. Flattered, but not interested. Probably married, too.

With a groan of disappointment, I stepped away and unzipped my parka. *Might as well get comfortable, even if I do have to spend all of my time alone.* "Fine, then. Yes, I would appreciate an escort to dinner." If I didn't have one, I'd likely get lost in the snowstorm, not able to tell up from down.

After a quick nod, he lifted his hood and left. A cold breeze rushed in during the quick moment the door stood open and a chill ran through me. Shivering, I considered zipping up again, but decided to dive under the covers of the double bed. *Or maybe a hot shower would be better.*

Shucking off the bulky layers, I headed for the bathroom, desperately needing something to warm me up. After opening the door, I wanted to slam it shut again.

Fuck, fuck, fuck!

No shower. Just a damn toilet and sink. No tub, I could understand, but was it too much to expect at least a tiny stall to wash up in? *This is turning out to be the worst vacation ever.*

I rushed to the bed, not worrying if anyone spotted me naked. It wasn't as if anyone could see *anything* with the snow flying around. Diving under the covers, I yanked them up to my chin, willing a way to stop the shakes tormenting me.

The usual haunting vision of Todd fucking another woman crept into my mind, but I shoved it aside. I didn't need him making this trip worse. Besides, I had fresh fodder from my guide to fantasize with. Interested or not, he couldn't stop me from imagining him licking my pussy or pounding into me with what was sure to be a gloriously large cock. Liquid fire rushed through my veins, forcing away the chill.

I drew a finger along my slick folds, picturing my guide between my legs, his tongue darting in and out of me while he rubbed my clit with his thumb. Pleasure I'd craved for so long.

Reaching over the side of the bed, I tugged open the nightstand drawer, hoping for something cock-shaped to fill me. I gasped when I saw a long box with my name on it. Who'd left it, I had no idea. Slipping off the lid, I found a silver bullet vibrator and a huge dildo beside it, labeled

Goliath. A strange gift. But with my growing desire, I didn't care. The object would fill every inch of my pussy as I'm sure my guide would have.

After a quick trip to the bathroom to wash the items, I dropped the bullet into the larger toy and scurried into bed.

Imagining the weight of my own personal Thor on top of me, his lips sending me into a dizzying frenzy of lust, I shoved Goliath inside. My hips shot off the bed, and I cried out. *Holy shit!*

On his knees, he pounds in and slides out again, ready for the next attack. Over and over, each plunge ramps up the electric tension, filling me with nothing but need. I grab his thighs and thrust toward him, meeting him halfway. There is no slowing the pace, no relenting, just a mad rush for release. His grunts grow louder and he rams into my pussy, the force and the swell of his cock sending me over the edge.

My body twitches. The orgasm rips through me in shock waves and I draw him back down on me. In between raspy breaths, he melds his lips to mine, taking all I have to offer with his demanding kiss. Our tongues battle in an erotic war, neither one of us retreating. He rocks inside me, gearing up for another round. And I am ready.

More, give me more.

· · · • ✳ • · · ·

I woke; sure I heard breathing above me. After a few seconds, I opened my eyes, but found myself alone, the sun starting to rise over the horizon. I rubbed my face and reached for my watch. *Shit.* At some point during my fantasy, I'd dozed off, slept right through dinner and into the next morning. Goliath rested against my leg, his heavy weight leaving me yearning for the real thing. Sure, I'd had offers over the past year, but no one had gotten my heart racing the way Todd used to. At least, not until my Nordic guide.

Knock, knock.

"Come in." I hauled the covers up to cover my chest, unsure who stood outside, but hoping it was my guide.

A bundled-up person entered the igloo. Gloved hands tugged off the hood, revealing my fantasy man once more.

"Good morning, I...." His cheeks flushed more than they already had from the cold. "I'm sorry; I'll leave you to dress."

He turned around and I threw down the sheets and rushed off the bed, grabbing the edge of his coat. "No, please stay. What is it you came here for?"

"To escort you to breakfast." He remained facing the door. "You didn't answer last night at dinnertime, so I let you sleep."

"Wait, how did you know I was sleeping?" *What a missed opportunity.*

He dug the toe of his boot into the floor. "I came inside to make sure you were okay. When I saw you were asleep, I didn't want to bother you."

Jet lag must have really kicked the crap out of me if I hadn't noticed someone enter the igloo. "Okay, just give me a minute to dress." I shifted to stand in front of him, making sure he saw everything. "That is, unless you want to have some fun, first."

A spark lit his eyes, and he groaned. "I can't."

A better reaction than the day before, though still not what I wanted to hear. I cupped the mass of clothing between his legs and pressed my naked body against his parka. "Why not?"

"It's complicated." Gripping my shoulders, he guided me away from him, but not before I caught his gaze on me. "Besides, I'm working. Are you coming or not?"

"I'd love to be coming with you deep inside me."

Nothing. Not even a hint of a smile or a flush of his cheeks.

I rolled my eyes. "Okay, since you don't want to cooperate, hang on."

After a quick wash-up in the bathroom and donning multiple layers again, I followed him outside. I glanced up. Millions of stars blanketed the sky. Even though the sun didn't rise until ten, the snow reflected enough light to make it easy to see where we were going. "Hey, when did it stop snowing?"

"Late last night." He stopped and waited for me to catch up before taking another step. "Supposed to be clear nights for the rest of the week. Should be great for seeing the Aurora Borealis."

"Yes, the Northern Lights. I've never had a chance to see them." Mostly because they occurred in the North, a direction I normally avoided. Had I known the man existed up there, I'd have come sooner.

"They're beautiful...." His voice trailed off as if he'd become lost in his own thoughts.

We trekked on without another word, but the silence drove me crazy I wanted to know more about the guy, what made him tick, and how to get him in my bed. *First things first.* "Hey, what's your name? Thor, maybe?"

He paused and looked back at me, humor in his eyes. "Thor was the name of my father. Though many say I resemble the Thor you Americans watch in movies. But the man who plays him comes from Australia." He spread his arms out. "He could never handle this much snow."

I smiled at his deep chuckle. *God, I want him.* "So, what *is* your name?"

"Ay-rik." He bowed, one hand out and the other holding his chest. "Spelled E-R-I-C-H."

"Erich, I like it. Now I know what to call you in my fantasies."

His eyes seemed to bulge out of his head for a second. Then, with a bark of laughter, he shook his head and started walking again.

Geez, this guy is a hard sell.

Chapter Two

Erich dropped me off at a beautiful log building, the entrance of the Snow Restaurant, to go in search of another guest to escort. With most of the guests already finished with breakfast, I ate my *pannukakku*, a Finnish pancake filled with custard and topped with raspberry jam, alone. During the day, I only returned to my igloo once, to quickly clean up and grab more layers of warm clothing. I spent the rest of the daylight hours visiting the Ice Gallery loaded with small ice sculptures, as well as some very large ones, enjoyed a ride on a sleigh pulled by reindeer, and even dropped in on a wedding in the Snow Chapel. The entire time, I searched for the gorgeous face of my Nordic hero, just a glance to make sure he wasn't a dream.

By dinner, I'd given up looking for him, exhausted from all of the walking and fresh air. I sat at a table with guests I would have guessed to be around my grandmother's age. So much for snowbirds. *This* group headed north for the winter instead.

It took every ounce of energy I had to fork food into my mouth. My eyelids grew heavy, and I could not stop yawning. The chatter around me ceased. *Shit, did I fall asleep?* I wiped my cheeks, expecting to find food on my face.

A throat cleared behind me.

Spinning around in my chair, I came face-to-groin with a bear, or rather, a large man dressed entirely in black. Curly, dark locks hung across his forehead and black stubble highlighted his hard jawline. But it was his blue eyes that drew my attention. *He's not Erich, but they sure grow them big and sexy around here.*

"Ms. Chambers?"

All the women around me cackled as he said my name. "She's Glenda's granddaughter," they whispered. As if that meant something.

I nodded at the man, curiosity shoving away all my dreariness.

"I'm Alek, Erich's brother." His voice was even deeper than his brother's, with a heavier accent. "He asked me to escort you to the sauna when you are finished with your meal."

Sauna? I gulped. A little more public than I was used to. But, what the hell. I was in a foreign land with people I'd never see again. I'd meet Erich anywhere he wanted.

"Okay." I set my napkin on the table and stood. "I'm ready now."

"Must be nice to have an escort," one of the ladies said.

"Especially one so hot," another giggled.

If only they'd seen his brother. Though, I likely would have had to fight them off to claim him. And that's what I planned to do when I found Erich. We'd get sweaty from more than the heat.

"Where is your outerwear?" Alek glanced around. "You need to get it on before we head out."

A cold chill raced up my spine. "We're going outside?" I didn't want to trek out into the snow, not until it was time to crash for the night. If someone offered a room in the hotel, or one of the cabins, I would have gladly traded places.

"Yes, that's the only way to get to the saunas. No underground tunnels way up here."

Great!

After dressing in my winter gear again, I followed Alek out into the arctic air. Anything to meet up with Erich and make my fantasies into my reality. We reached the large wooden cabins, bigger than the restaurant I'd just left, in no time. Alek led me into the smaller of the two, closing the door behind us.

"In thirty minutes, it will be busy here with other guests. Until then, enjoy." He gestured to the left. "You may undress in the change rooms. There are towels there, too."

No use wasting any time. I started removing clothing before I'd entered the women's change room. Thirty minutes wasn't even close to long enough with Erich, but I'd take what I could get.

Inside the room, lockers and benches sat arranged on one side, with toilets, sinks, and even showers on the other. I planned to make use of the shower another time, but had a date with my superhero look-alike first. Grabbing a towel on my way out, I wrapped up in it and bustled to find Alek.

As he opened the door to the private room, he nodded. My heart raced. I'd never had sex with a stranger, but after the year I'd had, I refused to deny my need. Dropping the towel, I glanced around for Erich, my prize for dealing with the frigid temperatures and snow. I breathed in the honey-scented steam around me, the sweet smell driving my hunger. But the room lay empty, no one else on any of the benches or tucked into a corner. Disappointment clutched my gut and wrung it out like a rag. All my desire, my lust, flittered into the steam, disappearing out the vent. I'd gotten my hopes up for nothing. Better though than finding him inside with someone else.

"Is the sauna to your liking?" Alek peeked in. A blush crept into his cheeks when he saw me.

"I didn't expect it to be quite so empty. I thought Erich would be waiting for me." Snatching my towel from the floor, I covered my lady bits, tucking the top corner into my cleavage. As flattered as I was by Alek's gaze, I wanted his brother's attention so much more.

"No, he has other obligations."

"A wife or girlfriend, right?" *I should have known.* A guy as hot as him had to have a variety of women to choose from.

He shook his head. "Visiting the Elders."

The Elders of the Sami people, no doubt. The driver of the shuttle bus had mentioned the indigenous tribe. But with his lighter complexion, I never would have guessed Erich to be a part of the tribe.

"You want to join me, then?" I'd spent enough time on my own already. Any company was better than none. Though, I wasn't ready to get frisky with Alek.

"No, I made a promise to Erich, which I must keep."

"What promise?" I'd only been in Erich's company twice, and for way too short a time. What promises could he possibly have asked his brother to make? Especially concerning me.

"If you're not happy here, I can take you to the swimming hole."

Avoiding the question. Typical. It seemed everyone I knew only answered the questions they chose to, leaving me to figure out the rest.

"Sure, why not." There wouldn't be any swimming with the river frozen, anyway. *Might be nice to get to know Alek and learn more about him and his brother.*

Clothes back on, I passed the shower, making a note to visit the building the next day.

Outside, the sky had darkened, though light from the lamps along the foot paths and the moon reflecting off the snow kept the place bright enough to see where we were going. I followed Alek to a snowmobile. *Finally, I don't have to walk.* Though, a ride could only mean we had to travel a fair distance.

He started the engine and I climbed on behind him. I tried wrapping my arms all the way around his waist, but he was too big so I clung to what I could, unsure how fast he planned to go.

His chuckle vibrated through his clothing. "Yes, be sure to hang on."

He revved the throttle then took off with a snap. If I hadn't been hanging on to him, I'd have flown off and landed on my ass.

I leaned against his back, trying to shield my face from the chill wind. But the cold on my cheeks did nothing to snuff the warmth rolling through me. I don't know which fueled my need more, the hum of the seat between my legs or the sexy man in front of me. Being told I couldn't have Erich had left me hungry for Alek. *Grandma did want me to have fun.*

When the snowmobile launched over a hill, gravity lost its hold on me for a moment and I gripped Alek's waist even more.

"We're on the river now," he said, his voice muffled from his fur-rimmed hood. "Almost there."

On the river? Holy shit! I'd assumed it to be frozen over, but would it be solid enough to support us both *and* the snowmobile?

Unable to clutch onto him any tighter, I whimpered with fear. Then we stopped. No warning. I slid forward from the momentum and might as well have been molded right onto his back.

He slid off and helped me to my feet. "Okay, now remove your clothing."

I froze in shock, my jaw dropping before I finally found words. "Are you mad?" Had I missed something? If he wanted me, he could have had me in the sauna where it was warm. There was no way I planned on taking my clothes off while standing on a frozen river. I'd trusted the guy way too easily.

Alek pulled off his parka and kicked free from his boots. "Well, you can't very well wear all that if we're going swimming."

Crazy person! "Um, the river is frozen. No place to go swimming around here."

He stepped to his right near what looked like black pipes sticking up from the ground. He bent and lifted a hatch. "We're going down there."

"No fucking way." I dreaded swimming in ice-cold water, let alone descending into a tiny hole. *What if he closes it on me?*

"It's part of the Lapland experience; has healthy effects

on your body."

I shook my head, unable to speak, teeth already chattering at the idea.

"Oh, come on. Don't you have the polar-bear plunge in America?"

"Yes, but I'm not crazy or drunk enough to do something so stupid."

Alek stood in front of me and removed his shirt, revealing a broad, muscled chest. Charcoal-colored hair littered his pecs, and a happy trail led into his pants. "If you do this, I promise I'll make it worth your while."

Off came his pants, leaving him in nothing but black boxer briefs.

Worth my while...? I focused on the nearly naked man, the outside temperature no longer an issue. Alek may not have been the guy I'd originally wanted, but he'd offered more than his brother had.

"Fine, I'll do it. But you have to promise to go in first. And once I come out, I expect you to warm me up in my bed."

He thrust out his chest and nodded with a sly grin. "Deal."

My clit throbbed. I rushed him, leapt up and grabbed his shoulders, wrapping my legs around his waist. *Maybe I can have him without diving into the cold water.*

With a chuckle, he peeled me off and set me in the snow. "I admire your eagerness, but I want you to experience this first."

God, these guys have strong wills. I've thrown myself at both of them and yet they resist. Am I not their type?

Alek spun around and jumped through the hole in the ice. After a few seconds, he bobbed partially above the water, looking even sexier wet. He wiped the water from his face and focused on me. "You coming in, or do you want me out first?"

Chewing on my lip, I imagined fucking him in the tiny space. Something I'd never done before. "Give me a sec.

I'm coming in." And hopefully we'd both be coming shortly.

Stripping to nothing but my bra and thong, I never once felt the cold, too determined to get some action. I climbed down the ladder at the edge of the hole. When my toe dipped into the water, I let go of the steps, falling in.

Free-zing! My chest ached immediately, as if squeezed by a vise. I darted to the surface, gasping for air. The chill bit into me, penetrating every inch of me with raw talons. I couldn't feel my feet or my hands, couldn't tread the water.

"Get me out." I thrashed around, trying to stay above the surface. But I started to sink, falling into the frigid depths.

Cold, so cold.

I struggled against the bonds holding me flat, fighting for breath and freedom.

"Shh, Heather. I've got you. You're okay."

Okay? How was I okay? I'd drowned. Hadn't I?

A warm hand trailed along my side and I stilled. I hadn't drowned. No, I was in my bed, a hard body beside me. One with a very prominent erection pressed against my ass. *I might not have drowned, but I've died and gone to heaven.*

I slowly rolled over, hoping the naked man wasn't some dream, an illusion I'd created in my last moments. Alek stared at me, hard lines of concern etched around his eyes and mouth.

"Are we both dead?" I asked.

He shook his head, brushing hair away from my face. "I pulled you from the river. Brought you right here."

Glancing around, I caught sight of the bright stars through the glass above us. Not home, as I'd originally thought, but in the glass igloo. "I was sinking. I don't remember anything after."

"No, I made sure you hadn't swallowed any water and were breathing. But, you'd already gone into shock."

I snuggled closer, craving his warmth and so much more. "You saved me."

He closed his eyes, pinching the bridge of his nose. "Yes, but I shouldn't have had to. I shouldn't have made you go in. I'm very sorry."

I opened my mouth and closed it again, struggling to find the right words to say. Sure, he coerced me below the ice, but I could have said no. I'd let my desire get the better of me. Unfortunately, I had to almost drown to get Alek in my bed. "I guess I can forgive you, but I expect you to make it up to me."

"Anything. Just tell me what you want me to do."

Skating my hand between us, I grabbed his cock. Thick, long, and oh-so-ready. "I know one way; you can give me what you promised before I jumped into the ice water. We're both already naked. Your doing, I assume."

"It was the fastest way to warm you up, using my own body heat." He pried my fingers from his shaft, much to my disappointment.

"C'mon." I clung to him, chest-to-chest, my thigh over his leg. "I'm still so cold. Plus, you said you'd make the plunge worth my while. And from the evidence between your legs, I know you want to plunge into me."

My breath caught as he moved over me, pinning me to the bed. "You sure don't make this easy."

"And neither do you. Just take me already." How much easier could I get?

"Fuck." He flopped onto his side and yanked me against him, my back to his chest, his cock resting between the cheeks of my ass. After lifting my leg and settling it over his, he drew a finger along my pussy. "This is all I can give you right now."

I'd take whatever he was willing to give, hoping his limits changed the longer we spent in bed.

Alek rubbed along my opening and circled my clit. Heat pooled low in my belly, and I gripped the sheets. One way or the other, I planned to have his dick buried deep inside me.

He kissed my neck, grinding against my ass. Close to penetration, but not close enough. In desperation, I slid my hand between my legs and guided his shaft to my pussy.

As if on fire, he jerked away. "Dammit, Heather, why did you do that?"

"Because I want you to fuck me. How much more obvious can I make it?" Was the guy really so clueless?

"I can't. How I wish I could, but I promised Erich—"

"Promised him what? If it involves me, I deserve to know."

"You will find out soon enough." He sat up, letting his gaze travel across the bed, avoiding a glance in my direction. "Until then, you will just have to be satisfied with what I can do."

"And what exactly does that mean?" Was there a promise of something more?

"This." He laid me onto my back again and knelt between my spread legs, sinking two fingers deep inside me. Not his cock, but definitely better than nothing. Leaning down, he flicked his tongue against my clit. I drew in a much-needed breath, feeling more alive than I had in a long time. Alek's thick, talented fingers sent me rushing toward my pending rapture. Waves of anticipation rippled through me. Such erotic torture.

He pulled away and I whimpered. So close and yet left empty.

"Please don't stop." I reached for him, craving more. Longing for completion.

"You're killing me, Heather. I can't handle the temptation."

"Then fuck me already." If he didn't do something soon, I would take matters into my own hands. He could watch if he wanted, but I refused to let go of the pleasure without an orgasm.

"No, Erich would kill me."

"He's not h—"

Alek slipped a finger into my ass, cutting off the rest of my sentence. He worked my tight hole and sucked my clit into his mouth.

I burst within seconds, convulsing with jolts of ecstasy. A cry bubbled from my throat as euphoria took over.

Spooning me again, Alek held me close as my mind whirled. "Your body is very receptive. I look forward to exploring it more."

There it was again, the promise of more. But his soft voice made me feel heavy, exhausted, as if my orgasm had been a depressant.

I wanted more, longed to find out if I could push Alek's limits even farther, but I lacked the energy. My eyelids heavy, I let them close, sinking into the warmth of my bed and the body behind me.

Chapter Three

Waves of light flittered through my closed lids. Opening them, I reached up to grab whatever floated above me. Nothing. Just the sun shining through the glass roof. Stationary.

Had I imagined the movement? I glanced around, searching for a possible source. *Maybe a bird flew over and cast a shadow through the glass.*

No one remained in the igloo with me. Not even Alek, his side of the bed cold. He must have left after I'd drifted off. Yet there wasn't an indent from his head on the pillow beside me and the chain was pulled across the door. Not possible without someone having locked it from the inside. *What the hell?*

I checked the entire igloo—which took all of one minute—just to be sure Alek wasn't tucked away somewhere, though hard to do with his size, for sure.

Nope, completely alone. *Something weird is going on.*

An aura appeared to my left. Hovering over the bed like a cloud of multi-colored sparkles, each one reflecting the sun. I rushed toward it, trying to grasp a piece of the translucent object. But my hand slid straight through, only a slight difference in temperature indicating something did float there. Warmer, as if some kind of being perhaps.

I stared at the form, and it remained still, but I had the peculiar sensation it examined me, too. A tingling of familiarity traveled through me, as if I'd encountered the strange entity before. Though I'm sure I would have remembered.

The light circled around me. Slow. Its warmth penetrated my skin.

I shouldn't have been so curious, should have screamed from the touch of the strange encounter, but I couldn't help myself. It brushed against my nipples, sending a rush of desire to my belly. A moan escaped my lips. The thing was more than just lights. *It's alive.*

With the strength of a human hand, the energy pushed me down to the bed. Nearing, it covered me with a heavier force than I expected.

I drew a quick breath. "Please, whatever you are, don't hurt me."

The weight lessened, yet some force probed between my legs, touching here and there, but nothing more, as if waiting for a response from me. I had no idea what it wanted. Was it sexual, or just curious?

The energy switched its focus, stroking my temples, my neck, brushing across my lips. So very gentle, replacing my unease with a sense of calm. *It doesn't want to hurt me. If it did, it would have by now.*

My own inquisitiveness got the better of me, and I spread my legs farther.

The life form returned its attention to my pussy. With gentle ministrations, it caressed my labia then focused on my clit. My pulse spiked. *Sexual, definitely sexual.*

I lay at the mercy of this unknown life form, never more vulnerable in my life. And my hunger drove away any lingering fear.

A hard energy drove into me. I had no idea how it made contact with me when every time I tried to hold onto it, my hand slipped right through. But what felt like an obvious erection swelled inside me and I rocked to take it all in.

Full. I'd never fell so complete, almost ready to burst. Even Goliath didn't measure up. The sensation spread beyond my hypersensitive inner walls, the life form penetrating by mind, my very soul. It read my thoughts, my fears and dreams. In a matter of minutes, it knew everything about me.

A sweet invasion.

The being changed shape to resemble something more humanoid. Yet, it still flickered above me. A man-shaped cloud of lights. And deep inside my pussy.

Withdrawing its internal probe, the creature rocked above me, pumping it in and out like a cock, the tip hitting my G-spot every time.

My nerves buzzed. How did something with no solid form provide so much pleasure? Still unable to hold it, I gripped the bed sheets instead and enjoyed everything the life form gave. Heat balled in my belly, raging straight through each limb. A heartbeat later, I detonated, shock waves from the orgasm rocking me. The ecstasy continued, pulsing along my muscles.

Needing some contact, I reached out to hold the form again, and touched something solid. A body, not a combination of lights and air. Soft skin grazed across my lips in a kiss.

Flicking open my lids, I gazed into the eyes of a man I'd met two days earlier. I gasped. "Erich?"

The figure disappeared, returning to its previous shapeless aura and flew straight up. Right through the glass with a burst of light. Sparks rained over me, but the being—whatever it was—had vanished. Had that really been Erich? It would explain his strange behavior. And he would have learned of my desire for him when he invaded my mind. He'd know what I did with his brother. Yet, that hadn't stopped him.

I touched my lips, remembering the kiss. So gentle. Running my hands across the sheets, I searched for some evidence Erich had been there. In my bed. Inside me. But there was nothing. No proof of Erich or anything else. Nothing but my stretched pussy drenched in my own juices. Had I imagined the entire encounter? Just as I'd imagined Alek? *I don't think so.*

Anxious for answers, I dressed, needing to find Erich. But first, I would visit the sauna for a shower. Regardless of the recent encounter, I didn't want to confront the Nordic hunk covered in the scent of sweat and sex.

Nothing. Not one single sighting. I spent the next two days asking around to find out if anyone had seen Erich. Or even his brother. Except for the ladies I'd eaten dinner with when Alek had come for me, no one knew who I referred to. The men didn't work for the igloo resort, and according to the guest information clerk, nobody by their names had checked in or out as guests.

Unease left me antsy and unable to eat. At dinner on the second day, I sat at my assigned table, pushing food across the plate with my fork, but not one bite had made it to my mouth.

There is no way I could have imagined Erich and Alek, or everything I've done with them.... Especially Alek. I had the wet clothes to prove I'd been in the river. And no one else had been there to save me.

I set down my fork and relaxed in my chair with a sigh, lightheaded from lack of food, yet couldn't bring myself to eat. *I can't have made it all up.*

Sure, the cloud of light seemed far-fetched. *But Erich and Alek have to be real.*

"Everything okay, sweetie?" My table neighbor—the same from two nights before—rested a hand on mine. "Even in the dim light here, you look a little pale."

"I...." How could I explain that I'd seen things and people who shouldn't exist? "I think I have an extreme case of jet lag." The best explanation I could think of.

"Things can't be that bad. Aren't you enjoying yourself here?"

"I am. It's just that—"

"You've seen and experienced things you don't understand." She squeezed my hand. "Such is the magic of Lapland."

"I wouldn't exactly call it magic." More like the fantasies of an overtired and heartbroken woman.

She raised her eyebrows. "You wouldn't call them magical?"

"Them?"

"Yes, the beings from another galaxy." Lowering her voice, she leaned in closer. "They take multiple shapes. But I'll bet my next pension check that the one who came for you the other night is one of them."

I paused. Had I heard her correctly? "You think Alek is an alien?"

"Yes, and the other one you're looking for, too."

"How do you know?" Complete fantasy or aliens? I didn't know which explanation sounded crazier.

"You hang around with their kind long enough, you learn to recognize them, even in human form."

"You mean, you've been with...?"

She winked. "An old widow like me wouldn't fly up here in the middle of winter if it wasn't worth it. I can tell you, I've never spent one single night here alone. My mate finds me every time I come here. Doesn't matter how long I've been away."

I smirked, impressed the woman still found love at her age. "Sure, you're married. Or maybe just a boyfriend. But beings from space? Maybe that's what you and your mate pretend, but there aren't aliens on Earth. Not yet, anyway."

Her smile vanished and she shook her head. "Your grandmother never told you, did she?"

"Told me what?"

She stood and patted my shoulder. "I suggest you eat up. You're going to need your energy. Especially if you have two of them after you. The solar winds are said to be strong tonight, which is their favorite time to play." Without a backward glance, she left.

Play? Can what she said really be true? Are my two Nordic hunks really extraterrestrials?

I stared at my food. Energy. If my next encounter resembled those I'd previously experienced with Erich and Alek, I definitely needed some. *Best to be prepared.*

Chapter Four

Wisps of green danced across the sky, intermingling with blues and purples. I stared from my bed in awe, captured by the beauty of the phenomenon. Though it was my first night actually seeing the Northern Lights, they made the trip worth dealing with cold temperatures and snow. I wanted to say Erich and Alek did too, but doubts still lingered as to whether they really existed.

I moaned with a shudder. Regardless of whether the Nordic hunks existed, thinking about them brought desire to the forefront of my brain. I slid a finger along my slick, swollen pussy. *So fuckin' horny.*

But I craved the real thing. A real man, with a real cock. Not a dildo or some fantasy. If the guys I'd met really existed, I wanted them. Alien or not. I needed a good fuck.

Tossing the covers off, I lay naked on the bed, legs spread. "Erich and Alek, if you are real, I want you now. Take me. Fuck me. Make me scream."

Seconds ticked by. Then minutes. Nothing. A tear slipped down my face. *They have to be real.*

"Don't cry, my love."

I gasped and jolted up, sitting on the edge of the bed. "Erich?"

Still nothing. No more voices, no clouds of light. Not even a knock on the door.

Fuck! I'd imagined it all, so desperate to be with someone again, to feel desirable. Pulling the blankets over me again, I curled into fetal position. The vacation hadn't worked the way my grandmother promised. Sure, I'd gotten over Todd—sort of—but, I wasn't having any fun. If anything, I realized I needed professional help. Counseling. Maybe that was my grandmother's plan. Though, I was sure she didn't need to send me past the Arctic Circle to do so.

The bed shifted behind me. Compressed, as if by some weight. A shower of lights rained from the ceiling, and a clouded figure formed in front of me.

My pulse spiked. *No, don't do this again.*

I closed my eyes, taking deep breaths to calm my racing heart. *This isn't real. Just your overactive imagination.*

"Heather, open your eyes."

Shit. Erich, and sounding sexier than ever saying my name with his deep, gravelly voice. I squeezed my lids tighter. "Go away."

"And why would you want us to do that? You called us."

Alek that time, his voice behind me. That explained the weight on my bed.

"Because you don't exist. I created you to get over the end of a relationship." Saying the words aloud made it easier to believe.

"Oh, I assure you, we're very real."

The blankets lifted behind me. A hard, warm body straightened against my back.

A jolt of desire shot through me. "Alek."

Finally opening my eyes, I braced for them both to disappear. Instead, Erich materialized out of the cloud, lacking a single shred of clothing. A fairer version of his brother, he had the same hard chest with just enough hair to look manly. And sexually aroused. I really was dreaming.

He kneeled on the floor in front of me, drawing my hair away from my face. "Do I look real to you, Heather?"

"Yes, but...." I wanted to believe them, prayed they really existed. Yet, the lingering doubt still hung on. "How did you get in here? I know you didn't come through the door."

Erich brushed a hand through his thick, blond locks. "That's what bothers you? How we got into your igloo?"

"I...."

Alek cupped my breast, rolling my nipple between his

fingers. I couldn't help but moan, ready to grant them whatever they wanted, though my mind struggled for control.

"Enough, Alek." Erich reached across me and shoved his brother. "Give her time to accept this. Accept us. Don't forget your training."

"Training?" *In what? Pleasure? Or confusing the hell out of guests?*

"In connecting with the people of Earth," Alek said, his tone defiant.

"You....You're aliens? The lady was right?" *Fuck, I really am dreaming.* But, I didn't want to be. Not with those two hunks in my igloo.

"Our kind came to this planet over one hundred years ago. We live in peace with the people of Lapland, unable to return to our home. Yet, we have no desire to leave this area, finding the rest of the people of Earth too confrontational. We know exactly what would happen to us if world governments ever found out."

Explaining away my own fantasy now. Great! "Then why make contact with guests here? Why take the chance of exposing your kind to others?"

"Some people are more open-minded than others." Erich clasped my hand. "Those are the ones we contact."

"And if you make a mistake in your assumptions?"

Alek trailed a finger down my arm, sending shivers along my spine. "You're having a hard time believing what's right in front of your eyes. Who would believe you if *you* told anyone?"

Exactly. I stared at the set of Erich's jaw. Tense. Obviously the more serious of the two. But why?

"Is this what *you* want, Erich? It almost seems as if you're forced to be here, like you'd rather not interact with humans."

"No!" His nostrils flared. "It's not that." He rested a hand on my shoulder, his touch tentative. "Sorry. This is all new to me. You're my first human."

140

I leaned forward, his behavior making more sense. "Hence, you refused my advances the first day."

He nodded, moving to sit on the bed beside me. "I didn't understand what you wanted."

Smiling at his vulnerability, I brushed my hand along his jaw. "You did just fine this morning."

His cheeks flushed.

"And just so you know...." I gripped his shaft. "You're my first alien, too." With two naked, sexy males in my igloo, I'd wasted too much time talking. Whether real or not, I planned to savor every moment with them. In the morning, I'd deal with the repercussions of the fantasy.

Alek cleared his throat behind me. "I thought I was your first."

"No need to get technical." I grabbed his cock too, guiding the guys closer. "Now, why did you come to visit this evening? Perhaps for some alien mating? Plan to probe me?"

"Why, yes." Alek shifted to the edge of the bed on my other side, his hard body tight against mine. "That is, if you want us."

Being with one of them would be a dream come true. With both: a wild time. "Of course."

He placed a hand on my head and his lips met mine, drawing me into his world. The last time we'd been together, he'd restrained himself, but this time, he offered everything. Warm hands held me close. He plundered my mouth with his wicked tongue, driving my need higher, each sweep holding so much passion.

I drew back, overwhelmed by the magnitude of it. No one had ever kissed me like that. Would his brother be the same?

Glancing to my right, I saw not a human form, but a cloud of lights. I waved my hand through him. "Erich, please don't disappear."

His outline flickered for a moment before returning to the man I'd first met, disappointment etched around his eyes. "I was just about to leave you two alone."

Oh no, you don't. "You're not going anywhere. You're going to be a part of this, too."

"But...." He furrowed his brows as if confused.

"I've wanted you since that first day, and I'm not letting you go anywhere." No one had permission to leave in the middle of my fantasy. "Besides, there's plenty of me to go around."

On my hands and knees, I wrapped my lips around the swollen tip of his cock. Swirling my tongue along his shaft, I bobbed on and off. If getting head didn't convince him to stay, I didn't know what would. He held onto my shoulders, moaning as he rocked in and out.

Alek splayed his hand across my ass, using his thumb to spread my pussy juice to my puckered hole.

"Yes." I glanced back at him. "Two holes to fuck. One for each of you." I'd been fucked in the ass before, and I'd never forgotten the intensity. But would having two guys together feel any different than a guy and a dildo? I hoped to find out soon.

I returned my attention to Erich, and Alek teased my clit. I cried out around the cock in my mouth, my legs shaking. He'd stolen my control and left me writhing in ecstasy. I jerked away from Erich, fearful I might bite him. The tension broke and orgasmic fire raced through my veins. "Fuck, yes!"

I struggled to stay on my hands and knees, my muscles threatening to give way from the shock waves still shuddering through me.

Alek grabbed my hips. "What do you say, brother? Ready to turn her around and sample the other side?"

"There's something I want to do first." Erich lifted me up until I knelt, wrapping his arms around me. His lust-filled gaze nearly stole my breath away. His lips brushed over mine in a sweet kiss, so soft and gentle. Slipping his fingers into my hair, he took the kiss to a new level, so deep and primal, he drew moans of pleasure from me. For one so inexperienced, he sure had a skilled mouth.

I pulled away for a much-needed breath, our lips smacking from the separation. "Wow."

Alek reached around, palming my breasts. Placing gentle kisses across my back, he tweaked my tender nipples. Each brush and pinch across the sensitive peaks heightened my arousal.

I gripped Erich's shaft. "I want you to fuck me. I'm going to turn around and suck off your brother, but I want you deep inside me."

He obeyed. As I teased Alek's head with my tongue, Erich plunged deep into my pussy. I jolted forward, almost choking on his brother's cock.

After the initial shock, I found my rhythm, swaying between them. Sucking and getting fucked. Two guys. And they both took everything I offered.

Alek's grunts grew louder. He gripped my hair and thrust faster. His breathing grew ragged and the veins in his arms bulged. "No, no, no!"

One second a hunky Nordic man, and the next, a cloud of light, shooting sparks across the igloo.

I gasped. *What the hell?*

Erich chuckled, withdrawing from me and holding me in his arms. "We're both still learning."

I relaxed against him. Sex with aliens was all new to me, too. "Is there anything we should do for him?" The sparks didn't burn, just created a colorful display.

"No, he'll come around. Until then...."

Erich lay on the bed, drawing me over him. I settled onto his cock with a sigh of pleasure. With newfound confidence, he rocked me above him. And I was more than happy to give up control to him. I arched my back, enjoying the languid motion.

Leaning down to taste his warm mouth again, I fed from him, his energy like oxygen to my fire. His strong arms surrounded me. I felt nothing but him.

He shifted his hips, pounding harder. With every

thrust, he seemed to plunge deeper. But it didn't hurt. A sweet invasion, just as it had been with him the other morning when he'd been in alien form.

I opened my eyes, finding nothing but a cloud of color below me. "Um, Erich?"

He flicked into his human form again and the invasion retreated. "Sorry, I lost concentration."

I doubted that. His concentration likely veered from remaining as a human to finding his release.

He grabbed my ass, and a new force rested behind me.

"Are you ready for both of us at the same time?" Alek pressed a finger into my fleshy ring.

My breath hitched. "Yes, God, yes. Lube is in my suitcase."

"Lube?"

"Yes, lubrication. You're not getting in my ass without any." Alien or not, they had to learn the rules.

Alek found the bottle rather quickly. "And I put it where?"

"All over your cock and around my asshole." With each snag during the sex with them, I began to doubt the experience as being a fantasy. My dream aliens would be much more dominant and experienced. Though I didn't have time to think about the alternative.

After preparing me, Alek pushed inside. Jolts of pleasure mixed with pain raced through me, my nerves buzzing as the guys gently thrust in and out.

Erich brushed a hand across my cheek. "You okay, Heather?"

"Yes, never been better." Unable to collect my thoughts, I clung to him, desperate for release.

But, it wouldn't come. I closed my eyes, concentrating on the two cocks teasing my most sensitive areas. "Please." I begged for mercy, clinging to the edge of sanity.

Whispers of a foreign language invaded my mind, the voices familiar, but I couldn't understand them.

I opened my eyes. *Shit!* I was no longer lying on top of

Erich, but floating above the bed. Clouds of light surrounded me. Penetrated me.

"Um, guys? You're alien again."

Close your eyes and let it be. Erich's voice. Inside my mind.

Holy fuck!

Yet, I obeyed him, fearful I'd crash onto the bed if I didn't.

My heart thundered. Their touch grew more intense and a euphoric sense of pleasure filled every part of me. Retreating and pushing, they reached all the way to the depths of my soul.

We will love you forever, Heather. Will you let us? Will you love us, too?

"Yes." Tears trailed down my cheeks. That was all I wanted, to be loved forever.

Then everything changed. Gravity returned, pulling on me again. I clung to Erich, who had returned to human form. He stood, holding my legs around his waist while he and Alek pounded into me. Their cocks swelled inside me, and they grunted with release.

As their hot seed spilled into me, I screamed against Erich's throat from the frenzy of simultaneous explosions. Uninhibited satisfaction.

They slipped out of me and, while Alek held me from behind, Erich lowered my legs to the ground. He cupped my cheek, staring at me with his intense blue eyes. "I meant what I said about forever. Is that what you want?"

I nodded, tears brimming.

"Good. Tomorrow, we will visit the Elders. Until then, you need to rest."

Erich and Alek laid me on the bed. I don't think I could have moved without their help, feeling like jelly. With one guy on either side of me, I succumbed to the sandman, happier and more fulfilled than I'd ever been.

Chapter Five

I'd never expected to wake up with company, thought I'd only imagined our ménage. But even learning my most intense fantasy had really happened hadn't prepared me for our next moments.

The two men woke, stretching their gorgeous bodies across my sheets. My Thor and a much beefier Loki. Alek leaned over for a kiss. Hot and heavy, the sensual contact left my toes curled. Erich's kiss was much more sensual. With him, I lost and found myself at the same time. When he pulled away, he placed his palm on my cheek.

"As much as I want to make love to you again, we don't have time. We're to be married by the Elders at sunrise."

Married? The three of us? Or just me and Erich?

What I always wanted, but not so suddenly. Where was the ring? Heck, I didn't even need that. I just wanted a say in the matter.

Erich hurried me through getting dressed and bundled up, leaving me no time to question his intentions. I clung to Alek on his snowmobile until we reached out destination. *Not the swimming hole.*

And then I stood deep in the woods, Erich on my right and Alek on my left, the same way I'd found them in my bed that morning. The Elders situated themselves before us, not leaders of the native people, but those from another planet. A row of beings, their light glittering in front of me. Erich and Alek remained in their human shape—the only ones present in that form—during the ceremony, prompting me when I needed to reply.

"Now, it's your turn." Erich gently squeezed my hand. "If you agree to marry us, you need to nod and say *seon.*"

My pulse raced, my hands sweaty in the palms of my husbands-to-be. If I agreed. But, what did I know about them besides they were amazing in bed? I knew nothing of their family, their people. Heck, I couldn't even say that I truly loved them. I'd known them for less than a week. The only thing I remained confident of was their commitment to me. *Is that enough?*

With all of the attention on me, all the aliens waiting for my response, I itched, as if bugs tried to burrow underneath my skin.

I tugged my hand from Erich's, gazing up at him.

He frowned, wrinkles bracketing his mouth and eyes. "You still don't believe. I thought you were ready, hoped you were, but you're not."

Ready to date again, sure. But marriage? I'd lived with Todd for a year, and look where it had gotten me. These guys I hadn't even known for a week. "I want to, but...."

A gust of warm air swept around me and debris flew up into my face. I covered my eyes with my arm. When the wind settled, I found myself in bed at my igloo. Alone. No aliens. No sign of anyone ever having been in the igloo with me. I rubbed my temples as my head spun. How much of what I'd experienced had been a dream? I ached in all the right places, a feeling I definitely could not have produced myself. But where were Erich and Alek? Why had they left me? Or had I just fantasized my whole vacation away?

The sun had risen. A quick glance at my phone revealed it was time for me to pack up and return to New York. Back to work and the life I'd forgotten about for a few days. Every movement and motion to get myself ready to leave left an ache in my heart. I wanted my sexy aliens to be real, but I couldn't live in a fantasy world for the rest of my life. I had to face reality, every single dreadful bit of it.

Suitcase in tow, I headed for the shuttle bus. Each step ripped at my soul. Was I leaving behind my one chance at love?

No, it hadn't been real. Not the aliens, nor the sex, or

even the wedding ceremony. I'd imagined it all. A wasted holiday in my own little world.

Guess I shouldn't have watched Thor *and* Avatar *on the plane.* I'd created my own fantasy to cope with my heartbreak. And the cold.

I stepped onto the bus, taking a quick glance across the resort, hoping to see Erich and Alek for proof I hadn't made it all up.

Swallowing the lump in my throat, I found a seat. At the rear, away from everyone else. My grandmother had tried to help me, but the trip hadn't worked. I needed professional help. When I returned home, I'd make an appointment with the company psychologist. *Time to get on with living.*

One year later...

I stepped off the shuttle bus, gazing out across the expanse of snow. My return to the igloo resort. A chance to bring closure. Or maybe assurance that my time spent there the previous winter had not happened as I'd remembered.

While counseling had helped me get over finding Todd in bed with another woman, it had done nothing to make me forget about Erich and Alek. I guess I should have told my psychologist about them.

I'd considered discussing the men I'd met with my grandmother—the one woman who could confirm or deny what I'd experienced in Lapland—but she'd become sick while I was away. Comatose. She'd passed on a week after I returned, leaving her timeshare to me.

And no matter how hard I tried, I couldn't recreate the fantasy at home. I wanted to believe I'd made up the aliens, but a piece of me refused to accept that explanation.

I visited the check-in desk of the resort to let them know I'd arrived. Papers had already been signed with the lawyer to transfer ownership of the timeshare to me, but I wanted to ensure nothing had been forgotten.

"Miss Chambers. Yes, I have a package for you. It seems someone knew to expect you." The clerk handed me a small package. "You're supposed to open it when you've settled into your igloo."

"Thank you."

I hiked through the snow to the glass igloo I remembered. No one met me to guide me there or to take me for a ride on his snowmobile.

Inside my room, I shook the snow from my coat, removed the extra layers of clothes, and hung my winter gear. After moving my suitcase to the side of my bed, I changed into a cotton T-shirt and pants.

Settled under the bed covers, I reached into my purse for the latest mystery novel. No romance for me. No dildos or other toys, either. I didn't need anything to encourage the wicked fantasies of the previous year. My hand knocked against the item I'd been given at the desk when I picked up the book. I chose the box instead, removing the red ribbon wrapped around it. Only a small object could fit inside. A trinket, jewelry, or even coins. Maybe something my grandmother had left behind on one of her visits. Very few people had known I was there, only that I'd gone on vacation. As I lifted off the lid, my hand shook and a tear slid down my cheek. Had my grandmother left me something before she passed away?

Inside lay a folded piece of paper. A note. *Why not place it in an envelope instead?*

I pulled the letter out and set the package aside.

Heather,

We are very glad you returned to Lapland. After last year, we worried you would not return. We went about things all wrong and are very sorry. We would like to see you again, if you are willing.

The ring inside the box is made of material from the planet of our ancestors. Put it on if you want to see us again. If you choose not to, we understand.

All our love,
Erich and Alek

Was that some kind of joke? I glanced around, half expecting to find a camera hidden somewhere. I hadn't told anyone about the men from my fantasies. Somehow, someone had found out and sent me the note. *Ha, ha. Not funny.*

I peeked inside the box at the gift. Resembled a normal ring to me. Just a plain gold band.

My eyes burned with the onset of tears. I tossed the package and its contents back into my suitcase. *I don't need this shit.* I'd come to put them behind me, to prove to myself they didn't exist.

Fuck.

Sobs wracked me. I yanked the blanket over my head. Why would someone do this to me? I should have told the psychologist about the fantasy. By keeping it a secret, I'd made everything worse.

After a restless night, I woke with cottonmouth and stiff muscles. I stretched my back, leaning my head over the edge of the bed. Not enough to get rid of the aches. I gathered a change of clothes, careful to avoid the letter. Hopefully, a shower and breakfast would help. Then I'd spend the day outside, participating in activities I'd missed the year before when I'd spent the entire time in my fantasy world.

At the restaurant, I picked at my eggs and sipped watered-down coffee. I didn't recognize any of the guests. Instead, a new, much younger crowd filled the building, all buzzing with excitement. Maybe coming there had been a bad idea altogether.

The ladies from the previous year had been my grandmother's age, but the new group of guests left me feeling more out of place. I wasn't twenty-something anymore.

I pushed back my chair and stood. No point in playing with food I wasn't going to eat.

"Ms. Sinclair, wait."

I spun to find the check-in girl racing toward me.

She waved something in the air. "I have an envelope for you."

Not another one. "If it's from the same person who left the box, I don't want it. You can tell them to leave me alone."

She frowned. "No, it's from your grandmother. You were supposed to get it last year, but it got misplaced." She handed it to me. "I just found it behind a filing cabinet in the storage room. Thought you might want it."

I numbed. "Thank you. I...I'm sorry I snapped at you."

"And I'm sorry you didn't get that sooner." She gave a shy smile. "Enjoy your stay."

The trek to my igloo seemed to take forever, but I refused to read whatever lay inside with an audience. I'd likely break down crying. A lump had formed in my throat by the time I'd settled on my bed and I fumbled to open the envelope, but finally managed to get the letter out.

My dearest Heather,

I hope you enjoy your time in Lapland. It is a magical place that has brought me much unexpected happiness. I never told anyone, but after your grandpappy passed away, I found another man who made me very happy. Though, due to circumstances, we only saw each other once a year during my trips here.

He passed away last year, which is why I won't be returning. But I hope you find the same happiness I did. You deserve it.

When you were a child, you were so sure there was life on other planets. I hope you still feel the same way, because you were right. Always believe.

Love you always,
Grandma

I breathed in deep to loosen the tightness in my chest. My grandmother and an alien.... I'd always wondered why she'd never gone out with any of the many men who wooed her. She'd already found someone, a being from outer space.

I'd been offered the same thing. Not one man, but two. But I'd refused to believe, been too caught up in my own heartbreak to think I deserved happiness. *Oh, God.*

Yet, did I want to be with two aliens? Would one visit a year be enough? *Better than a lifetime of loneliness and regret.*

I dug through the suitcase and found the ring. It weighed less than my engagement ring had, and didn't make me feel any different. Would it really work to bring Erich and Alek to me?

Won't hurt to try. But what finger do I put it on?

They'd asked me to marry them. And I'd hesitated. I hadn't believed and was sent away.

I slid the band onto my ring finger. A fitting place for it. *Where it should have been for the past year.*

"Erich and Alek, come back to me." I had no idea what to say, only hoped they heard me. "I believe and I want to be happy with both of you."

I waited for their clouds of light to appear, to zoom in through the roof of the glass igloo.

And I waited....

Nothing. Not a single twinkle.

Knots tightened in my gut. I didn't doubt my grandmother's note. She would never make up a story like that. The aliens had rejected me, just as I'd done to them. Or maybe they'd found someone younger as Todd had.

My heart ached as if someone had plunged a knife deep inside. Could I really die from a broken heart?

A knock on the door startled me, and I'm sure I squeaked. Had Erich and Alek arrived? *No, probably just another note to get my hopes up before crushing them once more.*

The knock came again, more insistent that time. "Heather, are you okay?"

I gasped. I knew that voice.

As I raced for the entrance, my heart pounded. I slipped off the lock and opened the door. Tears fell and I grinned, never more happy in my life. "You came."

Erich stepped forward, pulling me into his arms. "Of course. We were just waiting for your call."

"I thought you'd come in your other form."

"No." He brushed a finger across my cheekbone. "We've spent the last year trying to stay in this form. As humans."

Alek slid in past his brother. He kissed my cheek then stood behind me, rubbing his hands along my arms. "So we can leave this place. Visit you, too."

"Really?" I wouldn't have to go a year without seeing them?

Erich nodded. "The Elders helped us find a way, thought it would be better for our kind."

A squeal of excitement bubbled out from deep inside. I couldn't hold it in.

"So, what do you say we continue where we left off?" Alek said.

"With the wedding?"

Leaning closer, Erich claimed my mouth, then moved away just as quickly. "If that's what you want."

"And after that...." Alek grabbed my hips and drew me against him. "We can consummate our marriage. Over and over again."

"Yes!" I dressed into my winter gear in record time and headed out the door. We rode the snowmobile into the forest where the Elders waited for us once again. When asked if I would marry Erich and Alek, I answered *seon*, ready to spend the rest of my life with my aliens.

ABOUT THE AUTHOR

Jessica E. Subject is the author of science fiction romance, mostly alien romances, ranging from sweet to super hot. Sometimes she dabbles in paranormal and contemporary as well, bringing to life a wide variety of characters. In her stories, you could not only meet a sexy alien or two, but also clones and androids. You may be transported to a dystopian world where rebels are fighting to live and love, or to another planet for a romantic rendezvous.

When Jessica is not reading, writing, or doing dreaded housework, she likes to get out and walk with her giant, hairy dog her family adopted from the local animal shelter.

Jessica lives in Ontario, Canada with her husband and two energetic children. And she loves to hear from her readers. You can find her at http://jessicasubject.com and on twitter @jsubject. You can also subscribe to her electronic newsletter at http://eepurl.com/eX1Zw.